Dialogues

in

Paradise

Dialogues

in

Paradise

Can Xue

Translated by
Ronald R. Janssen
and
Jian Zhang

Northwestern University Press

Evanston, Illinois

Northwestern University Press
Evanston, Illinois 60201

This translation has been funded in
part by the National Endowment
for the Arts.

Printed in the United States
of America

10 9 8 7 6 5 4 3 2

ISBN 0-8101-0831-3

Design: William A. Seabright

To

Zhong Ming

for discovering

the subject

Contents

Acknowledgments

I have incurred many debts of gratitude during this work. The support of Robert Vogt, Dean of Hofstra College of Liberal Arts and Sciences, and Hofstra's exchange program enabled me to spend a year at East China Normal University in Shanghai. There I met Zhong Ming, who started the project by translating two of the stories. Professor Richard Bodman of St. Olaf's College encouraged me to enter the field. My studies years ago with Guy Davenport gave me the eyes to see such work as Can Xue's.

Others helped more directly. Xin Tian-yu of the Shanghai Academy of Social Sciences helped me to contact the author. My students Huang Young and Chang Bei-jing provided important material; Jon Solomon delivered work yet to be translated. Andrew Kappel and Lee Zimmerman suggested improvements to much of the work; the results were refined and polished by Jonathan Brent, whose editorial suggestions and, even more, enthusiasm for Can Xue's stories have shaped the work. Jonathan and Frances Padorr Brent published translations of four of these stories in *Formations*.

Most of all, I am grateful to Deng Xiao-hua (Can Xue) for her openness, generosity, and friendship, as well as for the inspiring example of her creative spirit, and to Jian Zhang for her hard work, courage, and devotion.

Four of the stories in this collection have appeared in English translation in the following issues of *Formations*: "Hut on the Mountain" and "The Ox," translated by Zhong Ming, in *Formations* 3:3 (Winter 1987); "Skylight," translated with Jian Zhang, in *Formations* 5:1 (Fall 1988); and "The Instant When the Cuckoo Sings," translated by Jian Zhang, in *Formations* 4:2 (Fall 1987).

The stories in this collection originally appeared in Chinese in the following publications and were translated from these texts. "The Gloomy Mood of Ah Mei on a Sunny Day" in *Tianjin Literature* (June 1986); "Raindrops in the Crevice between the Tiles" in *Chinese Intellectual* (Spring 1986); "Soap Bubbles in the Dirty Water" in *Shanghai Literature* (February 1987); "The Fog" in *China Monthly of Literature* (February 1986); "Hut on the Mountain" in *People's Literature* (August 1985); "The Ox" in *Lotus* (April 1985); "In the Wilderness" in *Shanghai Literature* (August 1986); "The Things That Happened to Me in That World" in *People's Literature* (November 1986); "The Date" in *Qing Hai Lake* (February 1987); "Skylight" in *China Monthly of Literature* (August 1986); "The Instant When the Cuckoo Sings" in *Youth Literature* (April 1986); "Dialogues in Paradise I" in *Sea Gull* (January 1987); "Dialogues in Paradise II" in *Qing Hai Lake* (February 1987); and "A Summer Day in the Beautiful South" in *China* (October 1986).

"Dream of the Yellow Chrysanthemum" and "Dialogues in Paradise III, IV, and V" have not been published in Chinese and were translated from the author's handwritten manuscript.

Ronald R. Janssen

Foreword

A Summer Day

in the

Beautiful

South

In 1957 my father, as head of the "anti-Party clique" at the New Hunan Daily, was condemned as an ultrarightist and transferred to Hunan Teachers' College to reform through labor, and my mother was sent to Hengshan Mountain for labor reform. In 1959, the whole family of nine was moved from the newspaper's residential area to a tiny hut of about ten square meters at the foot of Yueyushan Mountain. We lived on an income of less than ten yuan per person. That was the time of nationwide natural disasters. Since my father had neither savings nor help from outside, the whole family struggled along on the verge of death.

Summer night was full of mystery. When the grasshoppers, long-horned beetles, and other insects started their chorus, the six-year-old went sleepwalking again.

The kitchen was at the opposite end of the yard. It was dark inside. Pushing the door open, I heard a strange noise. Someone was pacing the room. I squatted down and reached into the coal container to start making briquettes.

A muffled flapping sound came from the yard. That was my grandma driving ghosts away with a stick. Moonlight shone on her, casting enchantment over her wrinkled but firm face. Bending her hunched back, she made all kinds of queer gestures, and called me to follow. I went down the stoop in darkness. Grandma caught me with her cold hand, so I followed to her newly opened vegetable plot and squatted down. I remember that I was awake by that time. Her whole body looked furry in the moonlight. Several wisps of white smoke drifted from her hair. I believed that the smoke came from her belly.

"The earth is cool," she murmured. I touched it and indeed found it very cool. "Just hold your breath and listen: there is a sound," she said. I raised my blurry eyes and saw the clear night sky full of shining blue waterdrops; a soft yet distinct sound could be heard everywhere: "tit-a-tat, tit-a-tat." I recalled that I had thrown a doll into the brook on the mountain.

"A snake is coiling in the toilet."

I pulled at Grandma's black robe. She didn't move, but propped her chin on her hand in meditation. Her body smelled of hay and wood.

"If a python is after you, you should circle to its back because it can't turn around once you are behind it. I have an uncle whose lower body was entwined by a python once. He held back the blood from the wound and poured in a packet of arsenic that he had in his pocket. The python ate it and died immediately. I have buried a bit of food in case you are hungry." So saying, she dug up a root tuber of some plant and handed it to me after shaking off the dirt. We sat until the dew came. Then I fell asleep, watching the rain come down like crazy. The whole night sky turned dazzling. Waking up in the morning, I found myself in bed. I may not have been sleepwalking at all. This will forever be a mystery.

The toilet was a straw hut on the hill, fifty meters from where we lived. A lizard lay there in ambush. Often I had to go to the toilet at night, but cried in terror on the way.

"Zai-zai, oh, Zai-zai!" Calling my nickname, Grandma tapped with her stick in the distance while waving a piece of burning fir bark and coughing at the same time to boost my courage. "You should think of something red, bright, shining," she said, rapping on the wooden door. The grasshoppers and beetles were singing, and the crickets, too.

I don't like cricket songs because they are black. But the songs of the long-horned beetles and grasshoppers are bright, while those of the owls are also dark. Summer is bright. That's why I love summer best of the four seasons. Winter is pitch-dark and smells of camphor.

The family could not afford to use coal, so Grandma took the two younger brothers and me to rake straw and collect wood in the mountains. The sun was so burning hot that the whole forest crackled. Pine moths dropped down on us every now and then. When a red swollen lump appeared, Grandma would spit on it and rub it, saying "OK, now." She smiled craftily then, but the wound still burned with pain.

When the firewood filled the basket, Grandma would sit down to rest. She wiped the dense perspiration from her forehead and observed the sun with narrowed eyes. Then she started once again the old, old story: "We have an uncle in our family who got a vest from a monk. It kept him cool in summer and warm in winter. If I had a thousand yuan, I would buy that vest at once." My mind would drift away, though my eyes remained wide open. "The vest is not to be bought, but can only belong to a spiritual Master."

My grandma must have been a beautiful girl with delicate features. Even when she was old, her teeth were white and sturdy. She could break thin wire with a single bite. She was extremely resolute and steadfast, yet an aura of mystery surrounded her. She often started up from deep sleep to investigate some unaccountable noise, waving a stick to make a rattling sound. Once I asked her about it, but she denied it completely, winking her eyes.

She knew every kind of wild vegetable and mushroom on the mountain, and she ate the blackish cakes made from wild marijuana leaves. She told us, "The more you chew it, the sweeter it becomes, because your saliva contains sugar." I tried and it worked. She gave those mushrooms the most beautiful names: "steamed-bread mushrooms," "cool mountain mushrooms," "red shirt mushrooms," "princess mushrooms," and so on. Thanks to these wild vegetables and mushrooms, we all survived, except her.

Grandma died of dropsy caused by hunger and fatigue. Lying on the edge of the big bed, her body swollen like an oxygen pillow, her face pale as a winding sheet, her hollowed eyes shining with dazzling sparks, she told us repeatedly that two pretty white mice were standing on the pullswitch playing games. "Coming down! They are coming down! Catch!" she yelled, with tears gleaming in her eyes and cold sweat dampening her face. When she was quiet, she stared at the sunbeam on the windowpane and asked smilingly if we could remember the things that had happened in the summer.

"As a matter of fact, there is no ghost. I've never seen one in all my sixty years," she said to me, holding my hand. Her palm was wet and feverish, completely different from its usual coolness and comfort. Somebody sent her some ground rice chaff before her death, but she could no longer swallow it. All the sisters in the family divided it up and ate it. The chaff was so sweet it might have been Grandma's blood — blood also contains sugar. Our young lives went on because we drank Grandma's blood.

Grandma died, but I was not at all mournful. I still didn't know the meaning of death. In my mind, death was only something black and disgusting. The best way to deal with it was to forget.

When the red sun dropped behind the out-house, mist rose near the pond. I squatted down and listened attentively. I could always hear the footsteps, "tit-a-tat, tit-a-tat." The scorching air whistled. Every-thing in the universe responded to those solemn and mysterious footsteps. From the golden gate of the set-ting sun, clouds of bats swarmed out. My little face flushed with jubilation.

To this day I've kept the habit of listening, holding my breath until the footsteps resound in my blood vessels. Very often they vibrate in my brain.

Father wore eyeglasses. Whatever he did, he was cau-tious and conscientious and accomplished everything step-by-step. The steamed rice we bought from the dining room was far from enough for everyone. He found a way out by loosening the rice clumps in our bowls with his chopsticks and piling the grains into a little heap. Finally he would say with satisfaction, "Pile, pile, there is another bowl of rice." He took great pains doing this at every meal, piling and piling until everyone was joyful. When we had porridge, he taught us how to lick the bowl. "This is grain. It would be a pity to waste it." So we licked and licked time and again. We didn't even need to wash the bowls.

One day I saw him waving to me in the sunshine at the doorway. Tapping on a cup with his chopsticks, he insisted on our guessing what was inside. It turned out that he had fried some balls made of a dozen pumpkin blossoms mixed with a little flour. Each of us had a bite. It was tasty. After this, he kept asking, "Is it good?" until we all gave a positive answer, swallowing our saliva in hunger. For several days he was immensely proud of himself for his outstanding concoction. He had planted more than a dozen pumpkins behind the house. He took good care of them. Every day after work, he watered the plants with urine, doing artificial pollination. As a result, the plants were thick in stem and strong in leaf. Yet they never grew pumpkins, except for an occasional baby pumpkin the size of a fist. He was so astonished that he kept saying to himself, "Outrageous, utterly outrageous!"

He also had a plot of sweet potatoes and was very serious about it. After the family moved to the opposite side of the river in 1962, he asked my brother to borrow a cart to carry the sweet potatoes. He worried whether one cart would be enough for the whole plot and whether he should give away what remained. Brother came back with a whole cartload of potato vines and some roots. Father stared for a long time before he said, "Can somebody have stolen the sweet potatoes?" Brother denied it, telling him that there had been no trace of digging in the plot. Then could it be that brother hadn't dug deeply enough? It didn't seem so because he had dug about one foot deep in some places. Father had to repeat again, "Outrageous, utterly outrageous!"

Our bitter life came to an end after we had eaten up all of his better woolen clothes except for a fur overcoat which he had bought for three hundred yuan. He told everybody, "This is the only thing I have rescued."

By that time, I was getting weak from severe TB, so the family ordered a bottle of milk for me every day. The milk was a thin and tasteless water mixture. After I finished, Father would fill half the bottle with water and shake it hard. Then he would drink it in one gulp. Wiping his mouth, he would say, "The milk is sweet, it contains protein." Mistaking his meaning, I truly believed that eggwhites were in the milk. *

One day he came back with a wounded baby hawk. With great delight, he told us it had flown into the office and gotten caught. The creature had to be fed meat. But where was the meat to come from? Then he said that frog would be a good substitute. So we went out looking high and low for frogs. When we came home with one, he had already set the bird free, saying that it would starve to death if we kept it. "It tried to peck my eyeball!" he exaggerated.

Dan bai means both "protein" and "eggwhites." (Translator)

My father stood aloof from worldly success and had no deep contact with people around him. Every day he sat at his desk reading works on dialectical materialism, making circles and dots in the books. His copper-framed glasses became corroded and the lenses fell out. Once, finding a tiny hammer and a galvanized steel plate, he worked a whole day and succeeded in reforming the frame. He put the glasses on, but two pieces of iron were attached. He didn't care — on the contrary, he enjoyed his own labor, saying, "They can last at least ten more years!" Indeed, he wore the glasses for a decade.

He had a watch which ran half an hour slow. Now and then, he opened the shell with tiny scissors and did some repairs with special tools. He struggled with the problem for years. Yet the watch still ran irregularly as if it had malaria. He refused to give in but continued his repairs in high spirits. He even told people, "My watch was made in Switzerland. It is thirty years old. Where can you find such good watches nowadays . . . ? When I marched south with the Liberation Army, it dropped into a stream. As I couldn't see clearly, I almost lost my life rescuing it."

He suffered from athlete's foot and ringworm in his toenails. He always went to the drugstore for a kind of "Strong Ringworm-Killer Cream." He applied it with patience and trimmed his nails carefully. Every week he would spend a whole morning on the work. The razors and shaving brushes, absorbent cotton, cotton swabs, all the trash from the thorough cleaning —

everything was put in careful order. However, owing to his myopia, he cut himself painfully every time. His toes were always bloodstained and horrible to see. So far as I know, this labor has gone on for some thirty-five years.

"Zai-zai," he would say, "go and buy Dad a bottle of 'Strong Ringworm Killer Cream.' "

"You're forever using it, but it doesn't work."

"What are you talking about? I'm much better now! The only remaining rash is on the small toes. I'm going to wipe it out at once. One bottle is enough — no, just half of it will heal me once and for all."

Sometimes, when an acquaintance came, Father would chat while trimming his nails. In the middle of a sentence, his hand would tremble and immediately he would put cotton on the toe and it would turn into a bundle of blood. All of this did not interfere with his loyalty to "Strong Ringworm-Killer Cream." He was tenacious in his struggle. Because of this extraordinary indomitability, he is in good shape even today, putting up an unremitting struggle against severe heart disease by working out in set after set of physical exercises. (Doctors insisted that he could not pass his fiftieth birthday, but he is over seventy.)

During the Cultural Revolution, the "Revolutionary rebels" came to search my house, only to find two drawers of "Strong Ringworm-Killer Cream." One young man was startled and jumped back. For some time, he couldn't gather courage to pick up the medicine. Then he sniffed the jar. He opened the lid.

"What trick is this?" he asked seriously.

I grinned. "It's for applying on the feet. It's poisonous!"

He was so scared he hurled it away.

After Grandma's death, I heard adults talking about Father's having heart disease. In those dark nights, my little heart beat hard in my chest. I kept my ears alert to the snoring next door. A terror of loneliness and helplessness overwhelmed me. My heart twitched in tender pity. For the first time I had an odd, terrifying connection in my mind with the dead, silent, rolling mountains and sparkling stars outside the door. I dared not wake up at night, but forced myself back into sleep whenever I grew conscious. The next day when the sun rose and the sky shone with red, I jumped up and down barefooted, my heart full of jubilation.

With the start of the Cultural Revolution in 1966, my schooling was discontinued just when I graduated from the primary grades. All my sisters went to the countryside. My father was caught and put in jail. My mother left for the "May 7th Cadre School." The house was taken away from us. All alone, I was left in the dark, small room assigned to me. I once moved to a little room under the staircase on the other side of the river where it was more convenient to send things to father. In 1970, thanks to my eldest sister's help through some of her acquaintances, I found a job in a neighborhood workshop. I was an ironworker and then an assembler for ten years.

My father was rehabilitated in 1979 and started working in the Provincial Political Consultative Committee in 1980. I quit my job in the workshop to have my child and because the transportation to work was inconvenient. But my new job request was turned down by someone at the Consultative Committee and Office of the United Front. In desperation, my husband, who was a well-known carpenter, and I had to work out our own way. We brought home some tailoring books and started learning tailoring. My husband went to work during the day and cut and sewed at night. Often we went to bed at four or five in the morning. After three or four months' study, I started to accept orders. I have perfected my skill through practice. Now we are well-established self-employed tailors. My husband has also quit his job and taken over the business. As for me, I am in charge of the household, the child's education, and a bit of dress design. A comfortable family, not very well-off, but cozy and passable.

All of a sudden, I was thirty. Ten years of youth had slipped by in struggle. I believe that I have something to say about these ten years, and about the future. What I have to say is something beyond ordinary consciousness, beyond ordinary talk. I want to say it in the form of literature and imagination. Something abstract, something emotional condenses itself in me. I started writing, wrote a little bit every day, without any consciousness as to why to put it this way or that way other than to stick to my own paradise, to ponder repeatedly, and to enjoy myself. This resulted in "The Old Floating Cloud" and many other published and unpublished works, behind which is the emotional support of the beautiful southern summer, the blazing sun in the south, the light and ardent artistic conception. In my early years, I walked far and wide in the scorching sun, bareheaded and barefoot, full of joy and boundless daydreaming.

My friend A. is a sincere and educated man. One day he spoke of his willingness to die and his hope that his wife also would die. I was shocked. He rattled on and on complaining about his wife. But he is not at all like this. I can see that he has collapsed and is really hoping for his wife's death. He might have poisoned her if the law wouldn't interfere. . . . But he is not yet dead and is still living with his wife. He regrets bitterly having revealed his skeleton in the closet to me.

My friend D. is a delicate-looking woman with a strong mind. She has dried up since her marriage. She has become so cold, forever angry, shuffling to the store to buy soy sauce with the backs of her shoes worn down. . . .

My friend E. is planning to "rebegin" every minute. Every time I go to his house to borrow books, he chatters away about his scheme as well as his brilliant progress. His spirits are always suspiciously high. This is followed by his complaint about his bad environment, the interference of his family. Whenever he is about to turn out some unusual achievement, something unexpected happens and sabotages the whole thing. . . . He has a ferocious wife who slapped him in front of his parents and spat in his face, calling him a "swindler" and a "good-for-nothing" and saying she "has now seen through him." At present he is living alone, his wife has left him. He has stopped talking about books with everyone except me. But his voice is a little hoarse. His most recent program is a great work on the new problems of economic reform.

My cousin M. is weak and cowardly, and so is his wife. Consequently, their son in secondary school despises them and has walked out on them. His wife is now completely mad, breaking bowls at home every day and torturing M. in a variety of ways. When I saw him last, his eyes looked dull and stupid, full of misery and tragedy.

I would like to be able to say that my work shines with a brightness that penetrates every word in every line. I would like to reemphasize that it is the beautiful blazing sun in the south that has evoked my creation. Because of the brightness in my heart, darkness becomes real darkness; because of the existence of paradise, we can have the deeply ingrained experience of hell; because of universal love, human beings can detach and sublimate themselves in the realm of art. Only mediocre and superficial persons can neglect this.

The
Gloomy
Mood of
Ah Mei
on a
Sunny
Day

I t has poured every day since last Thursday, but this morning it suddenly stopped, and now the sun is blazing. In the yard the mud reeks in the heat. All morning I have been shoveling up the worms that worked their way out of the mud. Fat and long and pink, they crawl into the house wherever they find a crack.

My neighbor stands in the yard digging with a coalrake at a hole in the high wall, which he has enlarged every night since it first appeared. When the wind surges into my room through that hole, the wall groans as if it were going to fall upon our little hut. At night, in fear, I bury my head under my quilt; sometimes I have to pile suitcases on the bed to hold the quilt down. Only then can I get a bit of sleep.

Da-gou is playing with firecrackers at the other side of the yard. He inserts one into a hole in the tree and sticks out his big hips as he bends over to light it. His bottom is huge, like his father's.

"Hey," I call. "Are you crazy? Can't you stop shooting those things?"

He stares at me blankly with his grayish white eyes. Picking his nose, he dashes from the yard. Minutes later, I hear firecrackers exploding somewhere at the rear of the house. My heart pounds, and I go into my room and stuff my ears with cotton which I find in a drawer.

I married Da-gou's father eight years ago. In the five months before our marriage he visited my family every now and then. He would sneak into the kitchen as soon as he arrived and start discussing something furtively with my mother. They talked and chuckled, often forgetting to cook the meals. In those days my mother always wore an ink-black apron. Sometimes she skipped washing her face in the morning, and her eyes were swollen like garlic bulbs. But whenever he came, Mother's eyes shone with happiness. She wiped her fat hands endlessly on the black apron. Old Li (at that time I called Da-gou's father "Old Li" because I couldn't remember any other name for him) was short in stature. Despite the purple pimples covering his face, he had, generally speaking, regular features.

One day I went to the kitchen for something and saw him peeling garlic with Mother. Both looked exhilarated. Passing by, I touched his clothes. He jumped aside in fright and said, frowning, "How are you!" His voice scared me. Dashing in, I grabbed what I needed, then ran away. I heard my mother complaining behind me: "That woman is always contemptuous like this." He came many times after that. But when he arrived Mother shut him in the kitchen and locked the door to prevent my intruding. They would laugh and chat, making a big mess.

It was terribly hot in July, and the house was full of tiny crawling worms. One day he proposed. I was in the kitchen fetching water. All of a sudden he entered. Before I could escape, he started talking.

"Hey, you, any comment to make about me?"

". . . "

Then he asked if I was willing to marry him immediately. His face turned gray and his body twitched, making me feel most uncomfortable while he spoke. He found a stool and sat down. The stool was black and greasy. One leg was loose, and it wobbled when people sat on it. He tipped to and fro, rattling off reasons we should marry. Most important was that my mother possessed an apartment, and he would be able to live there, thus avoiding the need to look for another dwelling. Hearing that, I could not hold back my laughter, and I tittered into my hand. His face turned red.

"Why are you laughing?" he demanded, his face drawn tight in rage.

"I intended to write a letter, but instead ended up here listening to you for such a long time."

"Oh, so that's it." He seemed relieved.

On our wedding day, all his pimples swelled into blackheads. His red nose was hard and bright like a candle. Seeing his short, small body wrapped tightly in new clothes, I couldn't help feeling misery and regret. That day I wore a suit the color of pickled cucumbers and looked awkward.

I heard Mother commenting to others in the kitchen, "She's not at all worthy to be his wife. It's her great fortune that he picked her. I thought nobody would marry her. I'm the only one clear about the fact that he takes a fancy not to her but to my family."

Even at the merry moment of my wedding, she still wore her ink-black apron. Her hair was uncombed and her breath was heavy with garlic.

Our wedding was both quiet and dull. We had only three guests, who sat pitifully at the table.

I felt sorry for them. Old Li became excited without reason. Jumping up and down, he told several jokes, but the guests remained unmoved.

That day it was pouring rain. When I went to the kitchen for dishes, rain splashing through the window soaked my pickle-colored suit. Glancing out, I saw a thief come into the yard and steal a lump of coal from the pile under the eaves, then flee along the wall.

The second day after the wedding, Old Li started hammering in the corner. He moved in a whole houseful of wood and made a mess.

"What are you making?" I asked, planning to write a letter in the park. At that time I had a hobby of letter writing.

"Building an attic," he grinned.

That night when I came home, I found the attic finished. A dirty net hung in it.

"From now on I'll sleep here," he hummed from within the net. "I'm used to sleeping alone. I get scared sleeping with you. I simply can't sleep. It's more peaceful here. Any comments?

I mumbled a reply.

For three months he stayed in the attic, then moved back to his own home. From the beginning, Mother kept silent about his departure. Since our wedding, their relationship had cooled down. Mother stopped talking with him in the kitchen, and considered him a loafer, a man putting on a monkey show.

"If only I had known he was a good-for-nothing putting on a monkey show I wouldn't have let my daughter marry him at all," Mother complained to everyone she met.

I didn't really feel Old Li was gone. I still thought he slept in that dirty net, and I believed that one day he would start talking from inside.

He stayed away until I gave birth to Da-gou.

Before that I often saw him on the street. His purple pimples had cleared up, and he was better looking than before. He no longer wore the short, small suit but instead had on a loose windbreaker, and his face bore the joyful look of a bachelor. Married men are easy to distinguish with a glance. Their backs are bent, their bodies feeble, and they have no style at all. Old Li, I thought, had certainly become handsome as soon as he left home. What would he have been like if he hadn't married me?

After the birth of Da-gou, he started visiting again. He sneaked into the kitchen as soon as he arrived. After a while, Mother ran out in horror. She peeped into my room through a crack in the door. When I pretended not to notice, she rushed into the next room, picked up Da-gou, and dashed back to the kitchen.

A few moments later, I heard the familiar chuckles as in the past.

These "courtesy calls" lasted several years.

Once I went out to send a letter and met Old Li coming in the front door. Just as before, he jumped aside in fright and said "How are you!" making a frown. I lowered my head pretending not to notice and walked away.

By then Mother had restored their former closeness. Whenever he came, she carried Da-gou to the kitchen. She would cook some dishes for him. They locked the door for fear I would know, but I smelled the cooking. I could only laugh at their pretense of secrecy.

When Da-gou was five, Old Li stopped his visits. Mother hated me all the more, maybe because of this. She cleaned a storeroom next to the kitchen and lived there. I believe she did this in order to avoid me.

I hardly feel the existence of Da-gou. He was raised entirely by my mother. He is short and small like his father, and I always wonder if his face will develop purple pimples. He got into the bad habit of eating raw garlic, and now he always reeks of it. In the past he took refuge with Old Li and Mother in the kitchen, eating garlic. I often heard Mother praising his appetite. "This boy might become a general one day," Mother told everybody, thinking herself very clever.

Da-gou has never called me "Mother," but always says "Hey" just like his father. I feel panic for a long time whenever he "Hey's" me. This is the cause of my heart disease.

For the past three years nothing has been heard of Old Li, and I have not seen him in the street. I imagine he has become a capable, handsome, short but "manly" man, relaxed and high-spirited in his walk. It was clever of him to leave us.

The sun is about to set behind the storeroom. Mother is coughing again. She has been coughing like this for over two months. Perhaps she feels she won't stay long in this world. She has locked her door lest I disturb her. The neighbor is still digging the hole in the wall. The wall will certainly fall down if the wind blows tonight. My house will collapse.

Raindrops

in the

Crevice

between

the

Tiles

A pril is a rainy month," she thought, lying in bed. "After April comes May. That makes me feel better." In her mind's eye May was radiant and enchanting. Gasping, she imagined her lungs as something ragged, like a worn-out fishing net. Four basins with chipped porcelain rims stood along the wall. Raindrops leaking through the roof tiles jingled into them, and bubbles floated on top of the water.

"San Mao," she called to her daughter in a shrill voice. "Bring me the appeal."

Her daughter circled the table, and threw a wad of crumpled papers onto her quilt. The mother grabbed it and smoothed it with shaky hands. Her face flushed from excitement, and she moved her thin finger, jointed like bamboo, along the lines. Her greedy eyes made out the words with difficulty, her mouth wide open, gasping for air.

"I've discovered some problems," she said. Her eyes sparkled with high excitement. "There are loopholes in several places. For example, here 'About the above question' should be changed to 'Because of the improper handling of the above several questions,' and 'require to compensate for the losses' is too abstract, doesn't touch the real nature of the problem, and . . ." She kept her mouth wide open. Her eyes bulged, looking like goldfish popping to the surface in their bowl. "That's the root of my failure! I can never find an appropriate way to express myself, can't hit the nail on the head. I often write 'puppy' when I mean 'rat.' I have also found that the report contains fifteen 'besides,' eighteen 'abouts.' Recently I've grown to like repetition. It has almost become a habit." She gestured, running out of breath.

Without raising her head from her book, the daughter said, "I have a friend whose mother does not reside at home but found an attic somewhere else to live in. Later she became an owl, sleeping during the day and moving about at night. Often there's a heavy rain outside and a drizzle inside the house. The quilts have become damp. Getting into one is like crawling into a cave. Will crabs grow at the foot of the wall?"

"I am forever a failure, simply can't find a suitably expressive way." The old woman gasped and rattled on, "Now I can see three places where 'besides' can be omitted. This makes the whole thing clear at a glance. Don't you think it's much improved? I have a feeling it will get the attention of the authorities at once." She raised her head only to discover that her daughter was no longer in the room. The empty chair stood against the wall. The remainder of her voice drifted on the air, buzzing like an insect.

The rain became heavier. Two of the basins were full. A black beetle fell into the water that spilled over onto the cement floor. After a desperate struggle, it sank.

"My life is full of failures. The key is my failure to find the appropriate way to express myself. This room is as cold as an icehouse." She remembered San Mao mumbling "owl," "owl" the whole night through. As if in a dream, the daughter cried out, pointing at the sky, "You're an owl!" At that moment the mother was gasping for breath, almost stifled to death. She pondered a long time after that but still couldn't figure out how she had turned into an owl.

Now that she wasn't dying for breath many queer ideas surged into her mind. She let them carry her away and before long she was asleep. She dreamed of a stretch of blue sky. In the sky was an airplane whose body was transparent green, like a huge locust. She woke up thinking: *It is radiant and enchanting in May.* She heard Yi Zi-hua stomp into the room, jabbering about 'snails' or something. Her head ached so severely that she didn't want to move.

"So you hide in your shell and refuse to come out now?" Yi Zi-hua sat down rudely on the bed, her behind bumping against the old woman's legs.

Pulling back one leg and curling up her body, the old woman closed her eyes, trying to guess what kind of news she brought.

"The chief is still wearing the same old stuff." Yi Zi-hua's mouth hung open. She mentioned the chief's apparel every time she came because she believed that how he dressed mysteriously affected everybody's personal interests. "I have wasted a whole day." Her voice was as sticky as a leech.

To take revenge for Yi's sitting on her legs, the old woman opened her eyes and said wickedly, "I also intend to see the chief tomorrow. My problem will *certainly* get his attention."

Yi Zi-hua gazed tolerantly at her and shook her head in disbelief. She yawned and said, "The chief is still in his deerskin jacket." Yi Zi-hua glanced at the mother again as though blaming her for her hasty and exaggerating tone.

The old woman flushed. She began to explain herself with last-ditch determination. "My problem is clear at a glance." She gave a snort of contempt. "My failure lies only in my inability to properly express myself. If only I could become a little bit more flexible. . . . Isn't that true? Today I went over the appeal and found several improper phrases. I believe just one more effort and my day will come, unlike certain people whose problems *really* can't be settled." Her speech ended sarcastically because she couldn't bear Yi's sardonic and dismissive behavior.

"The chief still wears the same thing!" Yi Zi-hua sneered as she stood up. Her gaze remained fixed on the mother's face.

The mother felt that a leech was sticking to her face. Whenever Yi Zi-hua came, the mother felt the same leech on her face, and the feeling disappeared only very slowly. But in her mind, Yi Zi-hua was also linked with something warm and encouraging. Because of this, her blood wasn't fully frozen; in her ragged lungs some living fluid still circulated. She curled her legs up in the cold, damp quilt so that they reached her chest. On the table lay an open book. The chair remained empty. She got goose bumps recalling the "owl."

Her mind switched to the radiant and enchanting May when her legs would be warmed a little. She dreamed of cicadas singing, dreamed of the locustlike airplane in the sky, until it was dusk and San Mao dragged herself into the house.

"Yi Zi-hua came today. My problem will draw attention," she said, putting on an optimistic air. "The chief is also interested."

The daughter only snorted through her nose and picked up her book.

"The key is the manner of expression. I have to become more flexible," she said, uncertain whether she should change to a more confident tone. "In my opinion, the thing will certainly take shape in May."

The daughter raised her eyebrows, staring at the air as if reading. "Since my friend's mother has become an owl, she has been thinking about flying out of the attic. Crabs live in the rock caves, owls perch in the forest. Everything in the universe has its own position. If you want to fly out, please open the window."

The rain had stopped long ago, and the four basins were full. A little beetle at the bottom of one basin was motionless. The old woman assumed it had suffocated. "Wonderful," she said.

"What?" Her daughter opened her eyes in surprise, pretending to be offended.

"May is radiant and enchanting," she said, enjoying her soft, rhythmic voice. The expression "radiant and enchanting" immediately reminded her of the locust-airplane.

"But can crabs grow at the foot of the wall?" her daughter asked, her eyes narrowed. "I think it's possible. The owl flies out from the window and breaks its wings in the sky. It falls down to the street, dead. In the darkness of night, you never hear the crunching sound. Your sleep is too deep. That's the sound of grinding bones. I can't stand the sound, and I always want to move out."

The mother stared at the ceiling for a long, long time, until a big raindrop fell from the crevice between the tiles into the basin. "Plink-plink," the clear sound startled her.

Soap

Bubbles

in the

Dirty

Water

My mother has melted into a basin of soap bubbles. Nobody knows what happened. I would be called a beast, a contemptible, sinister murderer, if anyone knew.

Early this morning she started calling from the kitchen. Her shouting caused fits of bursting pain in my temples.

For the past year, she has slept in the kitchen. In fact, the house does not lack space. But she never stopped complaining that her room was as cold as an icehouse, her nose running and saliva dripping as soon as she started in. She called me "an unfilial son, torturing his old mother like this." The whole show would end with a loud wail. One day, God knows how, she found the old worn-out camp bed in the attic, where nobody had been for years. Her face lit up with delight at finding this "treasure." Immediately she set up the bed opposite the gas range in the kitchen.

"Mother, please don't. Be careful you don't gas yourself."

"Good God, son!" She patted my shoulder and said, "Isn't that just what you've been hoping for? You dream of it every night. I understand very well. Just wait patiently. You might get your wish someday."

My face flushed, and I mumbled something meaningless.

As if to demonstrate, she shut the windows in the kitchen noisily and propped the door shut with a stick every night before going to bed. Strangely enough she never got gassed. Sometimes when a headache attacked me at midnight, I would become suspicious that Mother might be dead from the gas. Throwing on a jacket, I would rush out. But the sow-like snoring I would hear even before reaching the kitchen told me she slept soundly.

However, when she used to sleep in the bedroom she would complain about a lizard stinging her. Half of her head would be numb. Then she would get up to ransack boxes and chests, and I would spend the whole night without sleep. Whenever I hinted cautiously about my suffering, she would fly into a rage, shouting, "What's this? Your faithful mother has to be deprived of even such a tiny distraction? Oh, my good heavens!" Then, howling and slobbering, she would shove her body against me.

In the kitchen, I saw her poking her pasty little face from under the black quilt. Spitting filth from her teeth, she said, "Send the gift to Wang Qi-you today. I bought it yesterday. It's in the closet." She smiled treacherously, as if she had cooked up some plot and was waiting for me to eat it.

Wang Qi-you is an assistant section chief in my mother's workplace. He has a daughter, a thirty-three-year-old spinster whose face is exactly like her father's, with a tiny mole on one cheek. My mother adored him and took every chance to fawn over him. Unfortunately, the chief assumed grand airs, looking cold and indifferent, disliking her, perhaps, because of her age and ugly face. After failures on several social occasions, she had a brainstorm and found a good solution: to give me to him as a live-in son-in-law. I had been to the chief's house once. Of course, all his family knew the reason I was there. They murmured in each other's ears, laughing grimly. The section chief was picking his ears with a special little spoon. His earwax filled a whole watchbox. The thirty-three-year-old spinster was sitting beside a huge fireplace snorting out a strange noise that resembled a collection of animals roaring in a cave. As soon as she opened her mouth, cold sweat soaked my body.

"What damned business do you have here? Hmm? Scram! My piles are acting up!"

My mother is indeed an iron woman. She stayed there about a quarter of an hour, talking and laughing, not turning a hair. She took out a packet of dried bamboo shoots and said, "My little son presents this to the chief." Then she walked out the door, keeping her head high in the public gaze. In the following days, she couldn't resist boasting and hinting in a suggestive tone that she had a "special relationship" with the section chief.

"I have sore feet, Mother."

"What?" She jumped from the bed, breaking a web newly woven during the night. The spider clambered away somewhere into the bed.

"Whenever I hear you calling me, I feel as if my feet were being sawed through to the bone, and my stomach gets upset. I might vomit at their house."

"Stop that trick with me!" she shouted, waving her arms. The two veins in her thin neck danced like fish. "I have expected this. You're simply running against me! You put the spittoon on the threshold so that I'd step in it and fall down . . . Good Lord, what's happening here!"

Pausing, she ordered me to bow my head low before her. She poked my head left and right, searching up and down, even jabbing the back of my head with her filth-blackened nails. Finally, she spit a mouthful of water in my face and declared, "Your scheme can never work!" After that she started drumming her chest and boxing her ears until she was out of breath. And just then, something happened.

The instant she raised her hand to beat herself, she overturned a cup of tea she had left on the windowsill yesterday. The tea splashed her face. She tried to dry it with her sleeves, but rubbing only produced white bubbles on her skin. And where she rubbed, the flesh became hollow.

"Mother, why don't you have a bath. Let me prepare some water for you," I said as if commanded by a ghost.

After pouring boiling water into the wooden basin, I hid outside the door. I could hear Mother mixing in cold water and cursing me, saying I intended to burn her to death. Then she fell silent, taking off her clothes, perhaps. My face turned pale from nervousness, and I was shivering all over. I heard a stifled scream, as though somebody were calling for help before dawn. After that everything was quiet.

I jumped from the stairs. My clothes were soaking wet, my nails blue, my eyes bulging. After at least an hour, I forced open the kitchen door with a hammer and dashed inside.

The room was empty. My mother's clothes were at the bedside along with a pair of slippers. I stared at the water in the wooden basin, a basin of black, dirty, soapy water, on top of which floated a row of shining soap bubbles, spreading the smell of rotten wood.

I let myself sink down onto a small stool. I cried for her dirty, thin neck and her ulcerated feet watering all the year round.

I didn't call the others until noon.

So people came, swarmed in, their stomping feet breaking one of the floorboards. They looked left and right, observing my swollen eyes suspiciously. Finally, they came to the kitchen. One bent down to study the water in the basin and even broke a bubble with his finger. He was a short man with long hair who looked like a thief.

"She disappeared after her bath," I managed to speak up, something surging up from my stomach. The spider wove a new net on my head. The crowd grinned at one another.

"The water is smelly," the long-haired, short man said affectedly. "Maybe something has melted there? Just now I gave it a jab and felt that I had jabbed the backbone of a woman."

"You might have jabbed the thigh," the crowd replied excitedly. Opening their blood-red mouths, they burst into laughter. The tiles on the roof jumped, and the walls gave out pitiful cracking sounds.

They flew out like a swarm of bees, dancing for joy, reveling in the short man's unexpected discovery. Some couldn't restrain themselves from pissing under the eaves.

After they had left, I sat for a long time, keeping my head low. Some cold leftover rice was in the pot. I had two mouthfuls, which tasted of soap.

"San Mao, San Mao,* have you sent the gifts?" Mother's voice came from the bottom of the basin. The rows of soap bubbles seemed to stare at me in the ghastly light.

I staggered out. It was pitch-dark everywhere. Several street lamps shattered like thieves' eyes.

"San Mao! San Mao!" the shouting from the kitchen continued in a rising pitch as if getting angry.

Suddenly, I felt an itching in my throat. After a forceful cough, my mouth gave out a bark and then another and another. People encircled me as I jumped up and down barking ferociously. I discovered a particularly disgusting old fellow who pushed here and there in the crowd with an idiotic smile on his face, his crotch all wet with urine. I charged and bit his shoulder. Tearing hard, I ripped off a piece of flesh. He crashed down, bleeding, like a pile of firewood . . .

*Many Chinese names are not gender-restricted; San Mao is the name of a female character in the preceding story and a male character here. (Translator)

The

Fog

S ince the fog came, everything has grown blurry and trembling. All day I stretch my eyes wide trying to see clearly, but doing so is painful. This damned fog is everywhere. Even the bedroom is full of it. From morning to night it surges in like smoke. The walls are damp. During the day it is almost tolerable, but at night it is quite horrible. The quilt, soaked with moisture, becomes heavy and stiff and makes a creaking sound. Sticking your hand inside the quilt would make you shiver. My family rushes to the storeroom, which is piled up with wet gunnysacks. An electric stove in one corner makes the room steaming hot. Mother locks the door behind her as soon as she enters. Inside, the crowd presses close, pouring with sweat until morning.

"I am dying for love of the color yellow. It simply increases my appetite." These words seem to issue from my father's neck, which floats up out of the fog. His huge Adam's apple bobs up and down; a patch of black hairs grows on top of it. His hipbone cracks when he rolls out of sight into the fog.

There are five people in my household. We eat together and watch TV together in family harmony. But that morning when I opened the door, I saw the sun turn light blue. It seemed to be wrapped in long, fine hairs. It turned out that the fog had been unusually thick the night before. All my family became shapeless shadows. What's more, everyone became hotheaded, eccentric, even frivolous. Take my mother. On the second day of the fog, she declared that she was walking out on the family. Her reason, she claimed, was unbearable physical pain. After she left, Father's legs withered into wooden sticks tapping on the cement from morning to night. He even whistled popular tunes.

My two elder brothers are completely mad. They rummage through chests and cupboards. Everyone knows that they raise rats under the bed, but they still put on an air of secrecy, fearing that others might uncover their tricks. They consider me a thorn in their flesh and yell at me. I get so scared I hide in the wardrobe. It is suffocating inside and the camphor smell is unbearable. I hear them screaming and howling outside, smashing glass. I have great pity for them. They suffer from a severe bone disease and can't walk normally, even though they are over twenty. In the past, to prevent them from getting into trouble, Father tied them together with a rope and fastened the other end to his waist. Wherever he went, he dragged them along behind. But then their real personalities suddenly emerged, and the two boys ran out of control. Yet they still feel frightened to death and break glass to reassure themselves.

I have been looking for my mother. I know she has not really left, but must be hiding somewhere nearby because every night when we are sweating in the storeroom, we hear someone dash into the house and make a clean sweep of the leftovers. Once when I dragged my damp feet toward the door, rubbing my overfull belly, I saw a faded ribbon hanging on the grapevine. It looked like a gray rat.

"That's the one she helped put on your hair when you were a little girl. Sad, sad memory." Father winked and jabbed at the wall with his wooden legs. The sun was melting away into the steamy air and turned into a crescent moon. Someone rushed past the grapevine, breaking the mud doorstep.

"Mama?" I grabbed at a soaking wet sleeve.

"Looking for an egg. I once raised two white hens. They were laying eggs everywhere. It came to me all of a sudden that I had lost my direction in the forest. There is a steep cliff over there. Mountain torrents rush to the bottom in an instant." She shook herself loose from my grip. Waving her arms as though at a loss, she hurried away, her hasty steps resounding.

Mother's body was soft in her clothes, as though nothing were there. Who knows, maybe it was utter emptiness inside her garment. Maybe what I grabbed was not her clothes at all. She mentioned something I had totally forgotten. She hadn't raised hens for twenty years. Why should she be obsessed with that idea?

No, it couldn't have been Mother in the clothes. She should be a heavy woman, dripping oily sweat all night. I can't imagine what would happen if she didn't perspire away the oil.

"Your mother," Father says, whistling, "is digging earthworms at the other side of the mountain. She is having an attack of fantasy. She has had the disease for over twenty years. She hid the truth carefully from me when we got married. Wait until the end of this fog. I plan to travel and do something unusual. I have quite a few new ideas for earning money. They are chirping in my mind like a flock of chicks. Can't go on like that for long or they might become real chickens inside." He bends down, then stands erect, over and over, stooping down and standing up again and again. I can't see his head.

"Father?"

"I'm involved in the business of collecting bronze. This is my longtime wish. It may turn out to be a new start. You?" He gives a snort of contempt. "How many times you have laughed at me. I felt so ashamed I sobbed quietly in the toilet. It has been like this for decades. You simply blew up whenever I intimated my talents and plans. You hypocrites."

Mother falls down under an old Chinese scholar tree, her eyes glazed like porcelain. I run over to support her thin, light body. I can see her face gradually turn blue.

"I have found an egg near the cave on the cliff. Just look." In astonishment I watch her stretching out her thin, empty claw. My throat tightens. "I'm chasing those fleeting white shadows. My chest is bursting with exhaustion."

"The fog has damaged my eyes. I can't see you."

"There are some human figures in the woods over there. Can you feel that?"

"How can I? It's impossible. My eyes are completely destroyed." Frustrated, I withdraw my arm from her armpit which is as warm as under a hen's wing. Instantly one of her ribs cracks and breaks.

"It's only a rib." Her blue face wrinkles, then she disappears on the other side of the tree.

Finally, Father starts out. All night he hammers in his room, and by morning he has made a huge wooden trunk. He tries without success to tie the trunk with rope. He becomes so irritated he smashes the trunk to pieces with the hammer. He shouts in a loud voice: "Where have I put my traveling bag? Oh, thief! Good-for-nothing! I have put up with this for forty-five years. . . . Return my traveling bag!" He chases my elder brother out and never returns. Later on, my brother tells me that Father has not gone traveling. Instead, he is staying in a run-down temple near the house and lives by collecting scrap paper.

"He is quite pleased with himself and blows out a piercing noise through a bronze tube. He often boasts to the women that he is a bachelor. His behavior is too frivolous." Brother finishes his remark indignantly while hiding a watch in his shirt. That watch belongs to my mother, but he wants to sell it to the secondhand store to get some wine to drink in the temple. He spreads the word outside that he will accompany his dear father all his life.

In the morning I am wakened by the noise of the crows. I notice that Mother is looking for something along the foot of the wall. She is bending over the ground, her wax-yellow face almost touching the mud. She seems to be taking pains to identify something. Her dry eyeballs rub in their sockets with a soft grinding sound.

"What the hell's wrong with the white hen?"

"I smell a kind of odor here. It is from the earth. I have spent the whole morning doing this. If it is not because of the fog . . . in every petal of the magnolia . . . and those fat cutworms. As soon as I woke up in the morning, I realized that the egg was gone, the one I showed you. It was real, wasn't it? I found it in the bushes by the Chinese scholar tree. So far as I can remember, there were three white hens, one of them had dark spots along the neck forming a very fine circle, almost unnoticeable. And the other two were pure white.

"Your father," she continues, "is nothing but an outergarment. In the past he came to my house wearing that garment and refused to take it off even when he went to bed. One night I gathered enough courage to touch it with my hand, only to find that there was nothing inside at all. I recognized the truth years later."

I decide to tell her about the watch. I explain with difficulty. My mind is blank. I simply cannot make myself clear, not the least bit. My words condense into pasty spots sticking to the front of my jacket. I try some question marks, exclamation points, to exaggerate, but all in vain. Mother is asleep. I shake her violently and demand, "Do you understand?" Her blue face is crawling with insects.

A grayish white semicircle is drifting near the door, popping in and looking about. A cloud of yet denser fog.

Hut

on the

Mountain

O n the bleak and barren mountain behind our house stood a wooden hut.

Day after day I busied myself by tidying up my desk drawers. When I wasn't doing that I would sit in the armchair, my hands on my knees, listening to the tumultuous sounds of the north wind whipping against the fir-bark roof of the hut, and the howling of the wolves echoing in the valleys.

"Huh, you'll never get done with those drawers," said Mother, forcing a smile. "Not in your lifetime."

"There's something wrong with everyone's ears," I said with suppressed annoyance. "There are so many thieves wandering about our house in the moonlight, when I turn on the light I can see countless tiny holes poked by fingers in the windowscreens. In the next room, Father and you snore terribly, rattling the utensils in the kitchen cabinet. Then I kick about in my bed, turn my swollen head on the pillow and hear the man locked up in the hut banging furiously against the door. This goes on till daybreak."

"You give me a terrible start," Mother said, "every time you come into my room looking for things." She fixed her eyes on me as she backed toward the door. I saw the flesh of one of her cheeks contort ridiculously.

One day I decided to go up to the mountain to find out what on earth was the trouble. As soon as the wind let up, I began to climb. I climbed and climbed for a long time. The sunshine made me dizzy. Tiny white flames were flickering among the pebbles. I wandered about, coughing all the time. The salty sweat from my forehead was streaming into my eyes. I couldn't see or hear anything. When I reached home, I stood outside the door for a while and saw that the person reflected in the mirror had mud on her shoes and dark purple pouches under her eyes.

"It's some disease," I heard them snickering in the dark.

When my eyes became adapted to the darkness inside, they'd hidden themselves — laughing in their hiding places. I discovered they had made a mess of my desk drawers while I was out. A few dead moths and dragonflies were scattered on the floor — they knew only too well that these were treasures to me.

"They sorted the things in the drawers for you," little sister told me, "when you were out." She stared at me, her left eye turning green.

"I hear wolves howling," I deliberately tried to scare her. "They keep running around the house. Sometimes they poke their heads in through the cracks in the door. These things always happen after dusk. You get so scared in your dreams that cold sweat drips from the soles of your feet. Everyone in this house sweats this way in his sleep. You have only to see how damp the quilts are."

I felt upset because some of the things in my desk drawers were missing. Keeping her eyes on the floor, Mother pretended she knew nothing about it. But I had a feeling she was glaring ferociously at the back of my head since the spot would become numb and swollen whenever she did that. I also knew they had buried a box with my chess set by the well behind the house. They had done it many times, but each time I would dig the chess set out. When I dug for it, they would turn on the light and poke their heads out the window. In the face of my defiance they always tried to remain calm.

"Up there on the mountain," I told them at mealtime, "there is a hut."

They all lowered their heads, drinking soup noisily. Probably no one heard me.

"Lots of big rats were running wildly in the wind," I raised my voice and put down the chopsticks. "Rocks were rolling down the mountain and crashing into the back of our house. And you were so scared cold sweat dripped from your soles. Don't you remember? You only have to look at your quilts. Whenever the weather's fine, you're airing the quilts; the clothesline out there is always strung with them."

Father stole a glance at me with one eye, which, I noticed, was the all-too-familiar eye of a wolf. So that was it! At night he became one of the wolves running around the house, howling and wailing mournfully.

"White lights are swaying back and forth everywhere." I clutched Mother's shoulder with one hand. "Everything is so glaring that my eyes blear from the pain. You simply can't see a thing. But as soon as I return to my room, sit down in my armchair, and put my hands on my knees, I can see the fir-bark roof clearly. The image seems very close. In fact, every one of us must have seen it. Really, there's somebody squatting inside. He's got two big purple pouches under his eyes, too, because he stays up all night."

Father said, "Every time you dig by the well and hit stone with a screeching sound, you make Mother and me feel as if we were hanging in midair. We shudder at the sound and kick with bare feet but can't reach the ground." To avoid my eyes, he turned his face toward the window, the panes of which were thickly specked with fly droppings.

"At the bottom of the well," he went on, "there's a pair of scissors which I dropped some time ago. In my dreams I always make up my mind to fish them out. But as soon as I wake, I realize I've made a mistake. In fact, no scissors have ever fallen into the well. Your mother says positively that I've made a mistake. But I will not give up. It always steals into my mind again. Sometimes while I'm in bed, I am suddenly seized with regret: the scissors lie rusting at the bottom of the well, why shouldn't I go fish them out? I've been troubled by this for dozens of years. See my wrinkles? My face seems to have become furrowed. Once I actually went to the well and tried to lower a bucket into it. But the rope was thick and slippery. Suddenly my hands lost their grip and the bucket flopped with a loud boom, breaking into pieces in the well. I rushed back to the house, looked into the mirror, and saw the hair on my left temple had turned completely white."

"How that north wind pierces!" I hunched my shoulders. My face turned black and blue with cold.

"Bits of ice are forming in my stomach. When I sit down in my armchair I can hear them clinking away."

I had been intending to give my desk drawers a cleaning, but Mother was always stealthily making trouble. She'd walk to and fro in the next room, stamping, stamping, to my great distraction. I tried to ignore it, so I got a pack of cards and played, murmuring "one, two, three, four, five. . . ."

The pacing stopped all of a sudden and Mother poked her small dark green face into the room and mumbled, "I had a very obscene dream. Even now my back is dripping cold sweat."

"And your soles, too," I added. "Everyone's soles drip cold sweat. You aired your quilt again yesterday. It's usual enough."

Little sister sneaked in and told me that Mother had been thinking of breaking my arms because I was driving her crazy by opening and shutting the drawers. She was so tortured by the sound that every time she heard it, she'd soak her head in cold water until she caught a bad cold.

"This didn't happen by chance." Sister's stares were always so pointed that tiny pink measles broke out on my neck. "For example, I've heard Father talking about the scissors for perhaps twenty years. Everything has its own cause from way back. Everything."

So I oiled the sides of the drawers. And by opening and shutting them carefully, I managed to make no noise at all. I repeated this experiment for many days and the pacing in the next room ceased. She was fooled. This proves you can get away with anything as long as you take a little precaution. I was very excited over my success and worked hard all night. I was about to finish tidying my drawers when the light suddenly went out. I heard Mother's sneering laugh in the next room.

"That light from your room glares so that it makes all my blood vessels throb and throb, as though some drums were beating inside. Look," she said, pointing to her temple, where the blood vessels bulged like fat earthworms. "I'd rather get scurvy. There are throbbings throughout my body day and night. You have no idea how I'm suffering. Because of this ailment, your father once thought of committing suicide." She put her fat hand on my shoulder, an icy hand dripping with water.

Someone was making trouble by the well. I heard him letting the bucket down and drawing it up, again and again; the bucket hit against the wall of the well — boom, boom, boom. At dawn, he dropped the bucket with a loud bang and ran away. I opened the door of the next room and saw Father sleeping with his vein-ridged hand clutching the bedside, groaning in agony. Mother was beating the floor here and there with a broom; her hair was disheveled. At the moment of daybreak, she told me, a huge swarm of hideous beetles flew in through the window. They bumped against the walls and flopped onto the floor, which now was scattered with their remains. She got up to tidy the room, and as she was putting her feet into her slippers, a hidden bug bit her toe. Now her whole leg was swollen like a thick lead pipe.

"He," Mother pointed to Father, who was sleeping stuporously, "is dreaming it is he who is bitten."

"In the little hut on the mountain, someone is groaning, too. The black wind is blowing, carrying grape leaves along with it."

"Do you hear?" In the faint light of morning, Mother put her ear against the floor, listening with attention. "These bugs hurt themselves in their fall and passed out. They charged into the room earlier, at the moment of daybreak."

I did go up to the mountain that day, I remember. At first I was sitting in the cane chair, my hands on my knees. Then I opened the door and walked into the white light. I climbed up the mountain, seeing nothing but the white pebbles glowing with flames.

There were no grapevines, nor any hut.

Dream   One

of the

Yellow

Chrysanthemum

I t's ridiculous and shameful that Old Jiang would suddenly walk out on me. I should have discovered long ago that he would do such a thing. My life is full of such carelessness. One month ago, he found an ax somewhere and made motions around the old tree at the doorway as if measuring something. I was hiding behind the window aiming my air gun at a sparrow on a roof in the distance. I had been taking aim for two hours. But when I finally shot, full of confidence, the steel pellet zinged right into Old Jiang's arm. God knows why I lost my mind at the crucial moment. I was born with this impulsive personality. Immediately he jumped up and dashed into the room, shouting, "Murder! Murder!" I was totally embarrassed.

The whole business was carried out in secret. He always started work before dawn, when he believed I was sound asleep. He climbed up the ladder and chopped with the ax for half an hour, then wrapped the wounded tree trunk with a torn bed sheet and swept the ground clear of wood chips. Afterward, he would be jubilant the whole day, charging around the room on a child's bike. Here and there he threw a kind of waxed-paper plane he had made. He even tweaked my nose and asked in joy, "On such a picturesque spring day, what is your opinion of shooting pigs in the mountains? Do you believe that at a subtle moment in a deadly quiet night, some terrible crisis such as an earthquake might be brewing? During sound sleep, can one's nostrils puff out snow-white river sand?" After all that, he would force me to look out at the torn bed sheet, declaring loudly that it had flown onto the tree all by itself. "Whu-u-e-e-t! Whu-u-e-e-t! A two-whistle job! A real work of art! Unimaginable!"

My eyesight is getting sharper. Sometimes, I can aim for a whole day without blinking. Under such circumstances, I feel high-spirited and crystal clear; my heart beats strongly and my face is bloated with acne. In my proud mind, I have the desire to buy another child's bike and ride with Old Jiang. However, I get absentminded every now and then. Once I accidentally punctured Old Jiang's ear with a pellet. I was nervous for several days. I took the gun apart time and again, checking and adjusting, cold sweat drenching my head. At midnight, I got up and examined the tree with a flashlight. Bloodstained sparrows had sprouted all over the branches.

"One should have an accurate estimation of oneself," Old Jiang mumbled in bed.

Pointing my flashlight at him, I discovered that he was not awake. One pale, hairless leg was stretched outside the quilt. I touched it with my hand, but felt nothing at all. Streams of tiny insects were climbing up along the bedpost.

"What clouds and fog cover the target in the imagination?"

As a young man, Old Jiang used to shave his head. His hair smelled of celery all year round. His neck, on which no Adam's apple could be seen, stretched incredibly long. When we sat side by side on the bed, he could easily view what was happening outside the window simply by stretching his neck.

Then he would forget me and start a conversation outside the window. I would try to restrain his neck, but he would not even notice, talking as spittle flew into the emptiness. He walked with a soft, light step like an eel in the water. He called his walking "a symbol of tenderness" and felt quite proud of it. But what he admired more was his fingers. Those fingers were short and curved, and danced madly as if they had been electrocuted, constantly breaking bowls and cups. His fingers would frighten away a dancing partner. "He played tricks on my back!" the lady would say with hatred.

Every evening, he would wash those fingers with care and talk to himself at the same time. His voice was tender and puzzled: "What's the matter? Ah? I should treasure these darling fingers. Am I too careless? What a display of creative mind! Nothing compares with them without feeling humbled! Ah?"

One fall was particularly long and dark. I stayed indoors with him all the time. Heavy rain drenched the air with flowery fragrances. Through the gray windows, I seemed to see pale moths drifting in the drizzling sky. On the street, a fellow in huge leather boots was knocking like the devil at every window with a bamboo pole. Unconsciously, we sat back to back. The faintest movement would cause a cramp to the other. Old Jiang suggested that we dream of tree toads in the rain together.

"It's easy. My hair not only smells of celery but also of verbena. I dare not go out. I see the back of a mermaid exposed in the rapidly flooding pond every time I step out. When you were not in, the chairs and tables in our room danced in the air when the dulcimer started to play next door. I had to nail them to the floor. You ran out because you were haunted by your megalomania. In fact, nothing can be changed a bit. When you saw a person, your face felt hot and you were about to say something. But that was a sunny day. A gentle breeze bearing the fragrance of the yellow chrysanthemum wafted past. You paused and then forgot what you meant to say. You and I, we should have a dream of tree toads together. Water lilies blossom at our feet."

Guided by his urgings, I tried, but never dreamed of tree toads. Instead, I lay with my eyes wide open day and night watching numerous black holes open in the wall. The first sunny day after the long rain, we left the house, leaning on each other. We had forgotten how to walk. We had hardly stepped out when we fell into the mud and almost broke our bones. We couldn't open our eyes. We heard rabbits dashing past and the vast sea roaring. We dragged about until dark before crawling back home.

His mother died when winter was approaching. Before that, he had stolen two gold rings from the old woman. When people told him the news, he suddenly had the strange idea of keeping vigil beside the coffin. I sat with him in the pitch-dark mourning room, in fear that the dead woman would jump up to settle accounts. The oil lamp flickered, and a cold draft was sneaking under our feet like a snake. The coffin seemed to float in the air, creaking.

At night, some old women crept in, demanding, "Let's have some refreshments to pass the night! Let's have refreshments!" To cook, they lit a bonfire next to the coffin. The flame grew so high that the coffin caught fire. A strange smell spread through the room. Choking and coughing, I saw Old Jiang and the women ladle something from the pot to chew on. I looked carefully and was startled to see Old Jiang's mother sitting among them. Her eyes were half-closed, flowers were in her hair, and her chin rested in her hand. She, too, was chewing.

After a while, Old Jiang's emotion showed itself. Jumping up, he wailed. Then he kneeled down in front of each "mother," unburdening himself of his grief, clamping his head between his bony knees in bitter sorrow. I waited and waited. I was bored and so choked by the smoke I felt like vomiting. Finally, I stood up, hoping to get some fresh air outside.

"What trick are you up to?" Old Jiang caught me from behind. His look was as severe as iron; black spots appeared on his blue face. "Damn it, don't you have any conscience?"

The old women stared at me and then started whispering to each other. One pointed at me and then at the coffin, sneering. I rushed out of the room confused.

Many years later, on a fine afternoon, we sat with heavy hearts under a shaddock tree. One of our neighbors mentioned this incident. Old Jiang glared at me spitefully and said, "Too vulgar!" A white cat was lying at his feet.

Our connection to each other happened on a rainy day long, long ago. He had been a hanger-on of my family, a snakelike thing. You only notice what a nuisance such a person is when you are in quiet concentration. This situation lasted about ten years. Later on, we got married, because it dawned on me that he shaved his mustache every three days.

"It's funny," he said in a loud voice. The setting sun slanted through the window onto our clothes. Both of us felt warm and comfortable. Old Jiang said it was "the boiling of the ardent blood of youth." Then for no reason he picked up the vase and ended up dropping and breaking it into pieces. That was the first time I noticed his abnormal fingers.

"I have a goal." He stared at me for a long time before he spoke the vitally important thing in his heart. Holding my breath, I was ready to listen, but he dropped the subject and never raised it again. It might have been something extremely profound.

That day, the wooden wall of our room was crowded with armies of termites, marching to and fro, bustling with excitement. As soon as we climbed onto the bed, his gigantic figure disappeared under the quilt, leaving only his head sticking out.

"I don't occupy any space when I'm asleep. You won't mind this, will you? No mutual interference, that's my lifelong principle." His head rubbed on the pillow while talking, and he glared at me.

I doubted that his hair really smelled like celery. But the odor grew more convincing at his insistence. Eventually I believed I should consider it a fact. When I cautiously raised the issue, he spat on the ground ferociously, and said with disdain, "Too vulgar!"

The chopping of the tree came abruptly. Before that, he was listless for a long time, complaining that there was something flopping in his belly. He scoured all the medical books and asked me repeatedly, "Is there any example of male pregnancy?" Also at that time he gave me the air gun. According to him, this was something "elegant." He wanted me to train my "concentration" with it. Yet, whenever I raised the gun without his notice, he would scream as if from conditioned reflex, "Murder! Murder!" and flee without any trace. It happened every time.

Early this morning, I heard Old Jiang feel his way down from the bed. Believing that he intended only to chop the tree again, I pretended to be sound asleep. But I never heard the ax. I waited a long time before I got up and discovered that he had disappeared. Climbing the ladder, I tore down the bed sheet. The unharmed tree trunk appeared before me without even the faintest of scratches. At that moment, a breeze swept by with the odor of celery and verbena and with the fragrance of yellow chrysanthemum. Lowering my head, I saw thousands upon thousands of termites marching toward me along the ladder.

Where do the yellow chrysanthemums blossom?

Two

I dreamed of the crane at the very time Ru-shu had the same dream. That day, we were lying in the canvas sling chairs on the lawn. The mountain spring was jingling, a warm breeze was stroking our faces. Every now and then, Ru-shu bent down to catch a kind of white worm and rub it to death with two fingers. She watched so carefully when she was rubbing that the pupils in her eyes almost folded into one.

As the sun passed across her forehead, Ru-shu blushed and said, "Let's have a dream together."

So I saw the crane, a slender, pretty creature, full of aristocratic air. It circled the lake before it opened its wings and flew upward. When she awoke, Ru-shu told me she had had exactly the same dream. In her dream she even asked if I too was dreaming. My answer was positive. In her dream, too, there was a crane, and I became a gentleman in black, while she was wearing a purple gauze skirt. She made a detailed inquiry as to whether she wore purple in my dream. I couldn't answer because, strangely enough, in my dream there seemed to have been only the crane. In fact, I really hoped she would wear purple. Maybe one day, she would sit down suddenly on the lawn and start knitting. Over her head a huge pink umbrella would open.

"That crane is a good beginning," both of us declared. We were so moved that I patted her behind, feeling in my heart I had the strength to protect her.

Ru-shu's calling me "Old Thing" happened on our way home. Her pocket was lumpy. She said ambiguously it was the roses she had collected. But it was clear to me that it was the corpses of worms she had killed. "Old Thing," she said smilingly, "I believe that the arrangement of our room should be free of all vulgarity."

"My hair is very thick."

"The same. The name 'Old Thing' includes a certain sexual fantasy, just like a shaddock tree. . . ." She tried patiently to enlighten me.

It didn't take long for me to recognize her mad temperament. Every night she pressed me to re-assure her that I really had dreamed of the crane and really had answered her question in the dream. She bought more than a dozen pillows, piling up a hill on the bed. She would disappear into the heap as soon as the light was out.

From inside she said in a muffled voice, "Concentrate on one idea. The crane will land on the teapot. There you are in black and I am in a purple gauze skirt. We have been mediocre and unambitious all along. Shame on me. In the setting sun, we step into a white arch. The ground is covered with golden fallen leaves."

After a while, she started throwing pillows toward the ceiling. She made a terrible scene, rolling forward and backward. Finally, she jumped from the bed and turned it upside down. In the morning when she got up, she looked a different person with black rings around her eyes.

"My friends all say that I have a talent for swift judgment." She was scraping her thick mane of hair with hatred, observing me in the mirror, looking as though she were ready to explode with anger. "A complete waste." She gave a snort of contempt. "The moon is crescent then round, round then crescent. The blind man is walking on the long street. . . . "

In winter, we wanted some sun. Lying in our two sling chairs on the dried grass, we gazed into the distance. Far away there was a black hoist frame. I feared something, feeling that I had been shrinking and drying up every day. Ru-shu had her back to me, thinking by herself every day, one of her feet scratching letters on the ground. One day, she finally turned around and raised two whitened brows. As if nothing had happened, she said casually, "You mentioned some flower, now I have smelled it. It's nothing. I often see ocean waves and cliffs in my empty mind. Yesterday, I saw my face before death. Strangely enough, I had a tiny red flower on my temple."

"Chrysanthemum? I am drying up day by day!"

Bending down, she picked up those white worms and rubbed them back and forth in her palms, her brows pulled into a tight frown. Her palms were soaked with poisonous fluid and swollen like steamed buns.

"Every day at this time, someone hands a light blue fish, as slippery as an eel, through the crack in the door." She breathed hard on her palms, tears beading from her eyes. I cannot remember when we first saw a model plane made of glass. The plane circled us in the sun, giving out banging, explosive sounds. I felt a little chilly and hunched up my shoulders. Knocking my shinbone casually, I heard an empty, dry, broken sound. Ru-shu was sitting with her back toward me, scratching letters in the air. The gesture showed the arrogance in her very bones. About that time, she was painting the wall with yellowish brown sesame paste every day. When we were leaving, she wrapped up the dead worms in her handkerchief right before me. It made a big bundle.

The arrival of the old man was the turning point. I feel an unreasonable terror whenever I think of it. The morning when the accident happened, Ru-shu and I both heard the ocean waves. Ru-shu decided that the seven-mile embankment must have sprung a hole as big as a basin, and the seawater was rushing in toward the city. In the dim light, she bit open the pillows, twisting her body and groaning, "Bubbling, bubbling . . ."

He arrived at dawn. In his hand, he had a basket of dried unsalted fish. He dashed in, his body all wet. He dropped down on the bedside. With his head low, he searched in his basket, then peeped at me craftily. He said in a sarcastic tone, "In a certain rainy field, the chrysanthemums blossom miserably. I'm not saying this is a fact. It's only a kind of clue."

He slunk out when I was not paying attention. Furious, I tried to chase him to get a better explanation, but Ru-shu stopped me at the door.

She stared at the tip of her toes when she said, "What's the point in fussing endlessly? The thing is as clear as daylight. You know it yourself."

She gave a snort of contempt. Dashing over, she almost knocked me to the ground. I saw her pick up the binoculars from the table and focus at the back of the departing old man for a long time. Then she picked up the air gun and took aim. She fired a pellet, so gently that almost no sound could be heard. At the same time, her pupils expanded into two fine spiderwebs.

In the morning, I was shaving when she started talking behind me. I knew she was staring relentlessly at my back. "The tree toad gives birth to her sons in the bubbles. It's terrible."

Turning my head, I saw her hair covered with sweat, beads dropping to the ground. She started a story in a soft voice. In that story, a woman vomited blood every day.

"The pumpkin flowers are as brilliant as gold. One can escape the annoying glass plane under the tree's shade." Her neck became as lithe as a snake, full of lust. She stretched her neck saying, "Bubbling, bubbling. . . . "

I could hear the sea waves very near.

"Some people are shouting." I put away the razor.

Her face was emotional. "That woman is vomiting heavily, filling one spittoon after another. The disease started at birth. Both of us were walking on the embankment, one following the other, your shadow overlapping mine. We walked and walked, walked and walked. The sea waves were roaring under our feet. At the same time, the city was teeming with rats. I wanted to try my luck with the air gun."

"As a result, the old man fell down. You didn't even look at him." I said maliciously, "Your experiment was without result. As a matter of fact, you only meant to show off, to prove that you were not ready to give in. That's enough. Those skills are only your own creation."

Sure, there was once a certain fantasy! It was a conception of neither the crane nor the seashore. It often appears on the gray wall in the morning, or in the bright and tranquil mountains at noon. We cannot see it fully, but smell something that might exist and might not. At those moments, our bodies are full of energy, our nostrils expand. We stretch our heads out the window, looking around, completely at a loss. The odor can remain in the house for the whole day. Rushu becomes as tender and beautiful as a young girl, full of life and happiness. She finds the pink wool she put down ten years ago and says she will knit a "dazzling kerchief." Humming songs, she sits at the window knitting. Her fingers are as agile as shuttles working back and forth. Her pretty toes tap the floor restlessly. The whole day, she is motionless. With the approach of dusk, the world we are facing becomes grayer and grayer, more and more unreal. Unconsciously, I pinch my earlobes, which feel as thin as a sheet of paper, so I start to groan.

"Whenever I touch the scissors, I cut out an endless chain of high mountains." Ru-shu mumbles and wrinkles her tiny, sharp, grayish white nose. Raising her hand, she flings the half-done kerchief out the window.

The old man is forever a puzzle. When the window creaks in the autumn wind day and night, Ru-shu and I have endless thoughts about this. Our thinking slips toward one track. In front of us is a round tunnel. We have become so alike. Once we open our mouths, we say the same thing. Recently, we have found a clever trick: we stop talking, and instead, we only exchange understanding glances.

In deep sleep, the sweet-scented osmanthus drops onto our hair. Our hearts startle. In the golden sun come two young girls. Their eyelashes are long and soft, and sparks of yellow chrysanthemum burn quietly in the depths of their pupils.

The

Ox

I t was drizzling that day. In the wind, mulberries were falling from the old tree into the crevices between the tiles. In the big mirror on the wall I saw a purple light flashing outside the window. It was the rear of an ox which had just passed slowly by. I ran to the window and poked out my head.

"We are really well matched," said Old Guan hoarsely while rinsing the back of his mouth as if his throat were stuffed with hemp.

"The roots of the rosebushes are rotting; they've been soaked in the rain too long," I said uneasily as I withdrew from the window. "The petals have turned deathly pale. Did you notice last night that the room was flooded? My head must have been soaked in the rain all night. Look, the water is still oozing out from the roots of my hair."

"I'm going to brush my teeth," said Old Guan. "The crumbs of the crackers I ate last night got in between them. I'm feeling terrible. I swear . . . " Passing quietly behind me, he went into the kitchen. I heard him spitting out water noisily.

It came again in the afternoon. I was eating my lunch in front of the window when the familiar purple light flashed through a crack in the wooden wall. A horn poked through the hole — it had pierced the wooden wall. I stretched my head again and saw its smooth, round rump. It was going away. Slowly it moved on, crushing the cinders, which moaned mournfully under its hooves. Under the table, a swarm

of long-legged mosquitoes with white dots were at-
tacking my bare legs. For them that was a feast.

"I've just sworn," said Old Guan as he slithered out from the inner room like a cat, the gaudy
yellow patched sweater draped over his shoulders, "I'll
never eat crackers at night again. There are four cavities in my teeth. Two have reached the roots. You're
always afraid of mosquitoes and stamp your feet so
hard that the house seems to be falling apart. As a
matter of fact, you're too restless . . . "

"I've seen something," I told him vaguely. "A
strange purple color. This seemed to have first happened long, long ago."

"Look here," he was showing me his black
teeth. "These holes could have been dug by field mice."

Our bed stood against the wooden wall.
When I was about to fall asleep, the horn poked in
through the hole. I reached out to caress it, but what
I touched was the back of Old Guan's head, cold and
hard; it shrank and wrinkled.

"You tossed and turned in your sleep," he
said. "All night the field mice were scurrying between
my teeth like mad. Did you hear? I couldn't help eating
a couple of crackers again. Then I was done for. Why
couldn't I stop myself . . . "

"That thing keeps circling our house day and
night. Don't tell me you haven't heard it even once."

"I've been urged to have my bad teeth pulled
out. Then all my troubles would be gone, they say.
I've thought about it for some time but have decided

to keep things as they are, lest some other trouble should set in. I guess I'd better put up with it."

At dusk, there came the sobbing melody of a Chinese violin from beyond the hill. An orange glare shimmered on the windowpanes, hurting my eyes. Someone knocked at the door with three very light, hesitant taps. Perhaps it was only my imagination? I pushed the door open, only to see the round, smooth rump of the ox. The beast had passed by and was moving away, encircled in a broad aura of dark purple.

"Outside the hut where we used to live, there was a big Chinaberry tree. Whenever the wind blew, the dry, withered berries would fall down pit-a-pat." Old Guan was talking in his dream, agonizingly baring his teeth. He hadn't had any crackers for two nights. Every time he went without his nightly snack, he'd rave in his dream. "For years a white sheet had been hung under the tree. It was meant for wrapping up mother's body. Sure enough, it turned out to be very useful finally."

"One day," I too began talking, without realizing what I was doing, "I looked into the mirror and found that my hair had turned snow-white and a green secretion was oozing from the corners of my eyes. I thought of writing to a friend. So I went out to buy a bottle of ink. The south wind was blowing. I saw through the haze the blurred forms of children scurrying here and there in the wind. I tottered along, my hand on the brick wall for support. The road was slippery. Dust was blinding me, I couldn't see the house numbers . . . "

"The ground under the tree was covered by a thin moss with wretched-looking little flowers. Somebody had shoveled away the growth to dig for something underneath."

"My leg was crippled by mosquitoes. They were unusually ferocious that autumn. A big one bit me behind the knee, and ever since then this leg of mine has been crooked. Earlier I had been intending to buy some insecticide."

We talked all night. By morning we had blisters the size of soybeans on the tips of our tongues. The sun was shining warmly on our buttocks.

It came again, butting and bumping against the wooden wall, making a loud noise. I opened the door and was forced to shut my eyes by the dazzling flash of purple light.

"It has gone," I dropped my hands in disappointment. "It will keep circling us forever. Cold sweat is dripping from my armpits."

"Whenever the wind blows, many, many sentimental thoughts come into my mind. Take yesterday, for example. It suddenly occurred to me to preserve my decayed teeth in a jar of water. As I examined the cavities, I recalled some bygone incidents. You were looking into the mirror then. You're always looking into the mirror. It's surprising that you should care so much about your appearance."

It has not come since yesterday, when I stood at the window the whole day, combing my short hair, which is parched like hay, with a broken comb. In the pane, I could see clumps of hair between the teeth of the comb.

The wind swept away a few tiles from our roof and the rain leaked through, pitter-pattering all over the room. Old Guan and I took shelter in our bed under a makeshift canopy of oilcloth. The cloth sagged downward as a pool of rainwater collected in it. Old Guan curled in a corner of the bed, picking his nose, apprehensive and lost in thought.

"It hasn't come since yesterday," I told him. "Those things happened long, long ago — the mulberries that fell into the crevices between the tiles. There was a rattlesnake hanging from a branch. . . . Whenever I see purple, my blood boils. I've just bitten a blister on my tongue and now I taste nothing but — ugh — blood."

"What shall we do if our room is flooded? I wonder if the glass jar under the bed will be washed away. I have six teeth preserved inside."

"The roses outside are beaten down by the rain. This you must have heard? Someone wearing boots passed through the rose garden and left deep footprints. One day I saw you in the mirror trying to fill the cracks between your teeth with arsenic. Why?"

"I wanted to poison the field mice. They torture me. Is that why you're always looking in the mirror? I've been fighting these mice for years. The doctor says I have a superhuman will."

His lips turned black; his eyelids drooped heavily. He swayed and his skin suddenly wrinkled up like that of an eighty-year-old.

As I stretched out my hand to feel his brow, my fingers were pricked by bristly hair. Again he turned to me, baring his teeth in a comic expression of threat.

I went to the window and suddenly that day in May came back to me. He entered the room, supporting my mother with both hands and reeking of sweat, with a zebra-striped dragonfly resting on each shoulder.

"I've brought the scent of the fields," he told me bluntly, revealing his shiny white teeth. "The dentist says I show symptoms of decaying teeth. What nonsense!"

He was taking sleeping pills regularly then. Once he left a bottle of them on the table. My mother took them and never woke up afterward.

"The old woman had an odd fancy for western pills," he told the coroner.

I could see far, far away in the mirror. A huge beast had fallen into the water and was splashing and writhing in the throes of death. Black smoke was belching from its nose; dark red blood spurted from its mouth.

Panic-stricken, I turned around, only to see him raising a big hammer high above his head and swinging it toward the mirror.

In the

Wilderness

T hat night she lay down and suddenly realized she had not gone to sleep. So she got up and paced back and forth in the lightless room.

The rotten floor creaked gloomily underfoot. In the pitch dark, a yet darker form appeared stooping in the corner, looking like a bear. The thing moved, the floor creaked gloomily again.

"Who . . . " Her voice froze in her throat.

"Me." Her husband's frightened voice.

They were horrified by each other.

Every night after that they wandered in darkness in and out of the many empty rooms in the big apartment building, like two spirits. During the day she lowered her eyes as if she did not remember the things happening at night.

"The paperweight on the glass desktop is broken." Raising his bloodshot eyes, he stole a glance at her.

"How could it drop by itself? The wind at night is strong," she said. Lifting her shoulders, she felt a painful splitting of her ribs. "It's disgusting to sneak around like that!" she burst out unaccountably.

"There are snakes in some of the rooms, because they are shut and empty all the year round. Besides . . . " he continued, playing with a rubber tourniquet which was connected to a huge, brightly shining syringe needle. "Where did I stop just now? Oh, yes, one day a snake slithered along the baseboard. You should be careful not to be bitten by a snake . . . "

She had found the tourniquet and syringe needle under the pillow five days ago. It was brand-new and smelled of rubber. She had paid it no attention. But recently her husband played with it all the time. Even when asleep, he chewed on the rubber tube.

"You should go and listen to the weather forecast." He winked at her.

The room was large and empty. The north wind was banging the window, whose hook was gone.

To avoid bumping each other in the dark, both stepped more heavily.

He hung the tourniquet and the needle on a nail on the wall and left. She could smell the odor everywhere.

Coming back, he said, "I want to do an experiment. Let me catch a stray cat. This place is so huge and so dark. It must be a hiding place for all kinds of beasts. You know, I was wandering in the wilderness last night. The frozen rain fell heavily, soaking my back, freezing into an icy shell. Somewhere a strange step sounded. Who could have been walking there?"

"That was me walking on the other side," she said indifferently, leaning her swollen head into the shadow, trying to hide the dark rings around her eyes.

He stepped past and took down the tube and needle to play with. "Sometimes an unexpected turning point will occur." The tip of the needle sparkled in the flash of lightning.

She couldn't remember how long it had been since they had had any sleep. Every time she lay down, she heard that strange sound. Opening her eyes, she saw her husband biting the tourniquet with his eyes closed. The huge needle was inserted directly into his heart. She put on her clothes and stood up. Immediately, a dream pursued her. The wall was so damp her clothes stuck when she touched it.

"The paperweight is broken. Who did that?" he muttered from the corner, his mouth still gnawing.

"A dream is following me. It comes in through that small window. Like a shark, it swims in and puffs cold wind on the back of my neck. I haven't slept for days. See how wrinkled my skin is. Yesterday I broke the paperweight in panic trying to escape from that man-eater. How long will this chasing trick last?" Unconsciously she had fallen into complaining. "I can hardly tell whether I'm dreaming or awake. I babble at the office. My colleagues get frightened."

"Who is sure about these things? Some people spend all their lives this way. They cannot help falling asleep while walking or talking. Maybe that's the case with us."

"I'm so afraid of meeting people. They would recognize I'm in a trance. I try hard not to open my mouth at all."

He stepped into another room. She could still see the needle glint in his hand.

The thunder rumbled endlessly.

Ever since her childhood the apartment building had had so many empty rooms, large and dark, one after another, all in exactly the same design. She had never succeeded in counting them. Then he came. At the beginning, he planted Chinese boxwood on the windowsills and swept the room until the air was full of dust, his hair disheveled, his bottom protruding as he bent over. Whenever they had a guest, he would raise his voice, "The whole room is changed!" He never watered the plants, so they died. He threw them away, leaving only the empty pots on the sills. At night they looked like an army of skulls.

"It's worse than not to have planted anything," she complained, her waxen face looking discouraged.

"No plant can grow in such a place." He stamped with hatred. "A savage land."

He had stopped planting anything. Though young, he had started to suffer from asthma. Insomnia came unexpectedly. One day he awoke from a nap and noticed it was pitch-dark outside. Looking at the wall clock, he saw he had just lain down. He walked from one room to another, elbowing a pot off the windowsill. With a crash it hit the cement outside.

"Last night you broke the paperweight, the one with the lion's head. Why can't you restrain yourself a little?" He raised the topic stubbornly.

"The pots on the windowsills look so terrifying at night. Can't they be swept down?" She stopped. Her tone began to drift and float. "One day I'll make up my mind to throw them all down at once. It will be wonderful to see the windowsills empty."

He was so embarrassed his face turned red and his teeth clacked.

At night when they were dreaming awake, she noticed his feet stretch so long they became unfamiliar. The cold, bony soles touched her pillow. One toe was swollen like a carrot.

"You've taken up so much space," he mumbled in his quilt. "You're pushing me to the wall. The needle is on the wall. It's raining. You feel so happy. I am wandering through the wilderness. Suddenly, I step on a scorpion . . . "

She turned on the light. Her sleepy eyes were wide open. The needle was on the wall near the bed. A big drop of dark blood dripped from the point. The tourniquet was pulsating horribly, pressing the fluid inside. She went to the wilderness. Frozen rain was falling. The icy dregs shuttled from the trees. All her body was swollen. Water oozed from her swollen fingers. She wanted to sleep, but she heard someone groaning in the swamp. Clumsily, she moved toward the sound while dozing, muddleheaded. Small puddles cried out in pain beneath her feet.

He really had stepped on a scorpion. The toe swelled. The red, swollen spot expanded toward his knee. The puddles rippled in the wind. His leg stuck in the mud and refused to come loose. In the solitude, he heard the horrifying step come near.

"This is only a dream, a willing dream!" he protested. He was afraid of her approach.

The next step stopped near. But there was no one. The wilderness was empty. The step was in his imagination only. The imagined step stopped next to him.

An invisible hand hurt his toe. There was no escape. Icy cold hairs stood on end like thumbtacks one after another.

The clock broke after it struck the long strike. Wheels flew toward the sky like a flock of birds. The twisting rubber tube stuck on the dirty wall. Splashed on the ground was a swoop of painful black blood.

The

Things

That

Happened

to Me

in

That

World

To my

Friend

I t's midnight now, my friend. Outside the sky is pitch-dark. A heavy rain is falling. In the yard a noisy mob surges back and forth. Big raindrops thump on their oilcloth raincoats. They are digging up the camphor tree. Beside it lies a tung tree which was dragged here from far away. Last evening they charged into my house to discuss this. They talked on and on, clamoring, crying, jumping. At times they became so terribly suspicious that they began to search my house for something. A strong man, convulsed with excitement, shouted out, "So that's it. Plant a tung tree!"

"Plant a tung tree, ha ha ha!" they yelled madly. Slobbering, they fixed their eyes on me. Those eyes were culverts. The strong man carefully made a noose, and threw it toward my neck, blinking. "You, how dare you occupy this house?" His low voice was condemning.

Nor am I sure how I came here. All I remember is that it was snowing outside at first. The wide wasteland was deserted. Then the snow stopped. From the bluish white sky hung long, dazzling spears of ice. I lay on my back. I raised one finger. It was covered with frosty flowers. There were frozen cactuses and transparent reptiles in the wilderness. Delicate ice columns hung from the sky to the ground. I turned my head and heard a tearing sound, the sound of the ice growing into the earth.

Then they all came in. These people called themselves my distant relatives, and they said they had saved my life when I was young. Looking over their shoulders, I saw a line of mourners circling the bare hillside, human figures drifting up and down like strips of fine string. A bamboo flute appeared in the air every now and then, playing a tuneless, mournful melody.

"First of all, we must be rid of the camphor tree," the old woman at the corner of the door burst out. She was a hawk. Her body was wrapped in a black cloak. Her shoulders twitched, but her voice was as shrill as a chick's.

"Right, the camphor tree must be dug up," all agreed. Suddenly they panicked. "Can someone be overhearing us? Thieves are everywhere, nothing is reliable. We can't ignore this kind of problem. Ever since that windy day, there has been a crack in the sky . . . "

"We shall plant the tung tree!" they said firmly and emphatically, stamping their feet and crying out. With tears in their eyes, some rattled on about the yearlong terror and the coming prospects. After that they kicked each other about the back and hips and climbed up the window frame like monkeys, looking toward the distant hill in the dusk.

The black hawklike woman stealthily picked up a hoe from behind the door and began digging outside. A baby cried shrilly. Distant cocks crowed by mistake. Many cloth shoes ran in the dust. With a crash someone broke a bottle in the house.

I saw the flute in the mourning group pop up on the windowpane like a thievish eavesdropper. The strong man saw my glance. He dashed forward and covered the window with his back.

"Outside . . ." I started to say. I had been wanting to speak ever since they came in. I could no longer hold it back, as if forced by ghosts or gods. "In the pool on the limestone there is an eternal thing. When frost comes down from the sky, the dead water jingles . . . on the snow-covered ground lies a huge python, coiled like a snare . . . a gray figure bends down by the pool to salvage . . . "

They didn't hear me. To them, maybe, I had never spoken, but had only shaken my head and twisted my body strangely like an earthworm. They avoided me, cautiously tiptoeing around. The old woman even jabbed my waist with a knife-shaped pencil sharpener. Then she said to somebody, "So, it's stainless steel inside." She clicked her tongue. "Hush, be quiet! Someone is listening to us outside the door."

I shut my eyes and curl up in the corner. My friend, I was thinking of that ice mountain. If the sea thaws, the ice mountain will start floating. I raise my head from the water and see it move gently, like a solemn white whale in meditation. The icicle in the vault of heaven is dripping, tick, tick, tock, tick, tock. . . . A column reaching toward the sky breaks with a "crack." Flying pieces of ice draw arcs in a shiny, dreamy blue and then disappear in a wink. The rays of the icicle are eternal and dazzling. Have you ever had this experience, my friend? When your breast is open and your head becomes a reflective mirror, the stars are overshadowed. The sun pales into insignificance, flashing dimly in the darkness.

Raising my head from the water and shivering off the ice crusted on my forehead, I narrow my eyes. Frost falls from the sky. "There will be such a morning," I whisper to myself. "I will say, 'It is like this.'" Then everything starts over. The earth becomes muddy again. Under the huge, furry blanket vague desires and unusual disturbances will grow. The plants will be suffused with lascivious green . . . but I can't start over. I have already entered this world. The rays of the icicle are eternal and dazzling. The meteor is so stunned that it falls to the ground and becomes ugly stone. The silent snow peaks are shining brilliantly. I will stand still in this world, my friend. I am growing, growing into one of those sky-supporting ice columns. When that quivering reflection shines, I itch all over as if many sprouts and leaves were about to break through from inside. I move my neck and hear a gentle breeze whistle between the leaves. The full fluid flows under my armpit.

My eyes stare outside through the dirty glass.

The camphor tree has been dug up. The old woman leaps into the pit, giggling and laughing. She jumps up and down in the mud crazily. The others shovel mud down on her.

"Here is *another!*" The strong man suddenly points at my eyes inside the windowpane, laughing treacherously.

"Another one?" The group is startled, then, stirred up, they flee in all directions. The old woman buried in the pit is completely silent. She changes into a fossil.

I know they will come back to catch me in a minute. I fasten the door bolt and sneak into a huge wooden trunk and close the cover. I want to rise rapidly into the air. I want to change back to that ice column. I must hurry. This skin obstruction breaks open. Blood gushes as from a fountain. There isn't much time left. The mourners approach the stretch of wasteland. The north wind blows those thin strings into a tangle. At the other side of the swamp, a pack of hungry wolves is running. "Oh, oh, oh . . ." an old man sings. The vague noise is carried far, far away. To me he seems to say only one word: "String, string, oh, string . . ." And the strings become more and more entangled. The old man disappears, leaving the singing resounding at the horizon. The black flute is dumped with a clunk.

I hear the feet of wolves.

When the sea washes by, I explore my back rising out of the water. A strong, burning light expands my heart. I turn around, looking for the mirror. With a swift glance, I realize that my eyes have changed into violets. The pondering of the white whale is eternal. Chunks of broken ice collide with each other in the distance. There is no day and no night in the ice world. I raise my head from the water. I open my breast with great effort, spraying white sparks toward the outer universe. The ice peak gives off purple smoke, rolling deeply.

Of course, you know what this is all about, my friend. I am talking about that world, about icicles. Once long ago, snowflakes were falling from the sky.

We sang "Mom's Shoes" together, sitting at the curb. Then you knelt down and started to lick those white spirits. You said it was sugar. You froze your little face blue, and your fingers swelled up. In a flash of lightning I saw that time, but I hadn't learned how to convey it to you. When I finally remembered I should convey it, you had grown into a mature man. Your body was full of that sort of smoke. For years and years, I wandered around. I walked crazily along the river, dropping broken willow branches everywhere. Sometimes I stopped, casting my tear-blurred eyes into the distance. It was smiling at me but refused to come. Clumsily I sang "Mom's Shoes" from memory, calling up the ancient spirit. Day in and day out, year in and year out, it was hidden in the fog.

Then I stopped waiting. The relatives found me running to and fro on the river bank and believed something was wrong. They tied me up while I slept and shut me in a run-down temple. At night, ghosts and goblins cavorted, and underground something was jumping and running madly about. When they let me out, I was really beyond myself. My face was swollen, oozing pus from morning to night. My withered legs shivered. I would seize the sleeve of whoever passed by and say word by word, *"It is really fun at night."* My sunken eyes shone with malice, my fingers twisted and turned in my pocket. I also made a monkey mask and rushed into my relatives' houses, hugged them, and yelled, "It is really fun at night!" They examined me cautiously, nodded and exchanged whispered comments. I knew they had decided. They were waiting for a chance, like waiting for a hen to lay eggs.

A wide crack has been broken in the door. Someone probes this space.

My friend, it is time. Listen, the flaming hailstones are falling in a storm. The transparent tree is shaking its white canopy. The sea is waving carnally. Hand in hand we rise from the surface of the sea. We narrow our eyes, bathing in the radiance of the ice, and sing from our chests, "Mom's shoes . . ."

The

Date

T oday he had a date with me. He is the same type of person as I, the type I have created in my imagination. In recent years all kinds of people have made dates with me. They have all belonged to the type I have created in my imagination. Most often, I didn't go for the date in person. Instead, I had the rendezvous in my mind. But occasionally I went for the appointment, and brought back waxed-paper souvenirs. My bookcase is full of those colorful little things. I sit here gazing at them and all of a sudden can't hold back a chuckle. My husband always jabs at these trinkets with a specially made whisk broom pretending to clean up.

He invited me to go to a deserted island at three P.M. Then he added that I could refuse because it was not at all necessary. In fact, it might be too bad if I went.

I considered, and decided to go because it was not at all necessary not to go. It might be worse if I didn't. I had souvenirs on my mind when I made the decision.

The weather in the afternoon was not very promising, a little bit gloomy. A man stood at the other side of the street with a broken mirror, reflecting sunbeams on my wall which danced and circled dazzlingly. I put on a rat-gray trenchcoat and stepped out. I glanced around, dashed to the street, and sneaked into a taxi. Before I could open my mouth, the driver sped me to the island.

He was not there. The sun fell at a slant on the dry grass. A mud-colored locust whooshed into the sky, then fell into the grass. I'd been taken in. When the wind blew, tears ran from one eye, a sign of old age. It has been like that for a couple of years, and it is always the left eye.

The taxi was gone. I would have to walk home. I walked and walked. The wilderness was endless. A cold wind gusted, blowing my gray hair upright, patting against my face.

I could not leave the desert island. There was no way out. The glass sun disappeared. An incredible green light shone all around. It came from nowhere. The sky itself was pitch-dark.

I tried hard to remember. I recalled the taxi and its driver of vague appearance. But how could a car traverse the sea? Hadn't I arrived here directly? Somewhere in the distance I heard the waves and the whistle of steamships. I listened intently; nothing but fantasy was in my mind. My pocket watch was not working. Its works stuck so tightly it groaned and creaked and sweated like a human being, making the spot on my shirt wet through.

In the dim light, I realized he was there. His vague figure had its back toward me, bathed in that fantastic green light.

"Why have you come?" He still had the voice of an April morning, touched with the rasp of a cold.

"I want to see the sun rise." My dry lips swelled into fullness.

"You will disappear at sunrise. Why should you want to come?" he said again.

I suddenly realized I had never met him except in that house. A pocket watch hung there on the wall. He always met me at five in the morning. This had been going on for more than twenty years. When he came, he always kept his back to me and never turned his head. He had a broad back. At five o'clock, raindrops would beat on the palm leaves outside the window. He repeated the same sentence obsessively: "If the sun appears now, the beetles will change into helicopters." His footsteps were very light, and he always left at some unexpected moment. The door would shut; my neck would wither into wrinkles.

"Afraid I might miss your date, I often stay awake the whole night." I came near him and raised my eyebrows like a little girl. "The world is so wide. There are dark shadows everywhere. I walk back and forth through the shadows in my thin white nightgown. With my eyes wide open I gaze at my door. I'm afraid you will come while I'm asleep."

"We once strolled in the wilderness." I guess he smiled. "You were so light, but still you walked on tiptoe. You told me you were afraid of stepping on something and crushing it. I held your arms. There was nothing in my arms — you were as light as a wisp of smoke. Before dawn there was the strong smell of dried hay over the field. It was dark. Your white robe gleamed. You mumbled that it would be too bad to step on a frog. Groaning, you walked so fast I could hardly follow. Later, I abandoned you and retreated to the shadow of the city. I found real rest there."

"The green light has disappeared," I said softly.

Elephants glided here and there in the woods. Herds of deer were running in the distance.

From under the earth some muffled sound arose, calling, shivering the earth shell. The grass was ice-cold. The dew was about to fall. My pocket watch stopped. The broken spring was tangled in the case.

In the deep darkness I recognized him. He told me secretly how curved my lips were and how my eyes were bright as lamps. He said he had abandoned me then because he had been tired out. He had had to do that at the instant before dawn when the raindrops beat the palm leaves.

I too was tired out. When I ran barefoot to and fro outside, my soles were bloody with broken blisters. Without his realizing it, I leaned on his shoulder. "You always appear unexpectedly."

His shoulder became hot and powerful against my cheek. I heard a terrible spasm of his heart, blood bubbling over.

"There is no light at all."

"Now it is before dawn."

"The elephants have moved about the woods the whole night."

"You'll disappear at sunrise."

"How could I have recognized you? I have been imagining you like this for more than twenty years. But you are not at all like my imagination. Still I recognized you."

The dew was falling. My cloth shoes were soaked. I clung closer to him, secretly. My neck was slim and soft. I wanted to ask in detail about past decades, how he had searched for me, about that house, how he pushed open the door and entered, whether he had noticed the pocket watch on the wall. However, I had already forgotten what I wanted to say because the dew was thickening into drizzle. Wet through, I started to shiver.

"Everything will disappear at sunrise. You won't even have time to regret. I'll no longer appear in your room. You shouldn't have come. Now everything is ruined." His shoulder was turning cold on my cheek.

"I shall keep meeting you in my mind." Gloomily, I stopped shivering.

"The city is so large, but it is deserted at night. I shouted to you in the shadow. How could it be that you didn't hear? One morning when the mountain breeze was blowing, you sat at the window gazing at something, then you came out barefoot, your short hair scattered on your shoulders. Your white robe was covered with live golden butterflies, resting.

"My teeth are falling out. Listen: one, two, three . . . I am looking at you, and you have become a frozen shadow. The carmine seeps through my shrinking cheeks. That pocket watch, I have always kept it inside my shirt, near my heart."

Some night bird calls. His heart is frozen, blood is coagulating into big dark red blocks in his blood vessels. The dew on his mustache turns to frost.

He chews the ice between his teeth, then swallows with difficulty, moving his numbed lips. I guess he is saying, "Why have you come?" His eyes are open wide.

His eyes are full of vague dewdrops.

The first ray of sunlight appears on the horizon. His figure has condensed into mottled blocks. I cannot recognize him any longer. Drawing back his shoulders, he sits in silence. Then he groans heavily, rubbing his frostbitten heart.

The city is reawakening, shining and noisy.

He and I will live forever.

At dusk, the canary sings in the tree. We push open the windows in our separate rooms, collecting the evening mist into the rooms, indulging in the same ancient, obsessive fantasy.

Skylight

M y colleague's father burns corpses in a crematorium. He has worked as a cremator for most of his life, so his whole body bears a strange odor. One day his family secretly planned to abandon him. Since then he has been living in the small hut at the edge of the graveyard of the crematorium, all alone, as far as I know, for ten years. This morning I received an odd letter from him. It had no postmark, but instead a pencil drawing of a large skull. Strangely enough it reached my letter box with no trouble. The letter was peculiar. He wrote:

> It is fine here. The sky is blue and the air fresh.
> The air is full of fine-leaved Chinese mosla.
> Bunches upon bunches of grapes float in the
> mist. Every night there is a dance.
>
> Colleague A's Father

I got his point. I could imagine those grapes, their vines grown on the ashes of the dead.

Opening the window, I saw the heavy body of my mother squatting over the rubble. Breathing with difficulty, she was moving her bowels. Clumps and clusters of wormwood grew on the rubble pile. Mad with pain, she pulled them up and hurled them away.

All day I felt uneasy about the letter in my pocket. One of my younger brothers stole a glance at me several times and while we were drinking soup he slipped a rat dropping in my bowl to provoke me.

"Though this house is pretty old," Father intoned severely through his nasal cavity, which has been rotted into two tiny holes, "it's the only house in this area. Many years have passed by. I really enjoy our wormwood."

"Excellent!" My younger brother cheered up, spilling soup all over the table.

I don't understand why he used the word "enjoy." Throughout his life he has used such startling expressions.

They had seen through my thought.

At midnight the old cremator appeared in the mirror of the cupboard. He was a skein of vague stuff like a puff of air. He stretched his hand toward me from inside the mirror. It was full of the black smoke of burnt flesh.

"You've been waiting all the time?" he asked me. His voice was unclear and made sounds like a broken transistor radio. "We'll leave immediately."

Suddenly I remembered that I had made some sort of appointment with him.

Outside it was pitch-dark. He hastened forward five or six steps ahead of me, looking like an ape covered with hazy moonlight. Every dozen steps he reminded me, "Under our feet is a floating bridge."

At his reminder I actually felt a drifting sensation under my feet and heard running water.

"The fisherman fell into the hole before twelve o'clock," he said unaccountably.

I slipped. I clearly felt two rows of teeth biting my toes, then letting go immediately. I could hear hideous laughter beneath us, hateful cursing, hysterical howling. Amid all that noise, an alarm clock rang constantly. The old man walked as if on wings. I could hardly keep up with him for running out of breath. In the distance were two faint green lights. We dashed toward them with unimaginable speed. The closer we came, the dizzier I got and the more numb my feet felt. A creak, like a closing door. Everything disappeared.

"Come up." The old man was floating in the sky. His voice was still hoarse but combined with a shrillness from his throat.

I stamped lightly and rose up into the dark emptiness as he did.

Clack, clack, clack.

Clack, clack, clack, clack.

Clack, clack, clack, clack.

The sound of teeth gnashing reached us from all directions.

When my eyes got used to the darkness, I discovered quite a few fine lights swinging above the roof. In the faint light, I could make out that this was a straw hut about ten meters square. The walls were hung with fierce-looking skeletons.

"Those moving lights are time flying swiftly by." The old man gritted his teeth and rasped out, "Here the loneliness is ingrained. There's a spider's web in the corner. It's been there for twelve years. Twelve years ago my little daughter stood by the door and said, 'Pah!' I saw a huge tumor in her chest; it was pressing tightly against her little heart."

Clack, clack, clack.

The green light appeared again, two dots at first, then bigger and bigger, more dazzling, quivering, more soul-stirring than before.

"Hey you, get away!"

The light shrank back into two dots. A dark shadow brushed by, a clumsy night bird that shrieked and swooped toward the skylight, its huge wings tapping the roof fiercely, echoing like thunder.

"Man-eater," the old man said. I guess he was smiling. "It has miscalculated. When dawn comes, I'll take you to the skylight to see some wonderful things." He gave out a faint snore, but I struggled not to fall asleep. I was afraid that I might fall from the emptiness on which I was lying and drop into an abyss. The old man was rolling around all the time. His bones creaked as if the emptiness hurt his back. I tossed about most of the night. Later I saw the dew dripping shyly from the petals of lilacs. In the shining blue sky a gigantic red moon appeared like a furry monster. On the bare hill, thousands upon thousands of apes and monkeys shrieked to the monster in the sky. A peculiar, sweet fragrance filled the air.

"This is the odor of the fine-leaved Chinese mosla." The old man was already up while I was still sleeping on the pile of hay in the sky. Bending at the waist, he searched through the hay. His beard was full of straw. "The whole summer I have been collecting tiny grass. It piles up into a small hill at the back of my house. Why don't you go and have a look at my grapes?"

Before I had time to answer, he climbed to the top of the haystack and, jumping up swiftly, caught the windowsill of the skylight.

"Please climb up." He gestured to me and grinned mysteriously.

We rested the upper part of our bodies on the fir-bark roof. He elbowed me and pointed at the misty sky. "Please enjoy my treasures. Don't you see them? The brilliant pearls on the left? And on the right all the seedless green grapes?"

Grapes? Where? My God! I told him I could see nothing but fog. But he paid no attention to me.

"In the graveyard the lonesome gust blows all the year round. Sometimes it's accompanied by sand beating like a storm against the roof. Under the ancient cypress the wind sounds fierce and threatening. I've gotten used to standing alone in the wind. At that time the whole world is empty, except for an occasional old crow flying obliquely by. Just now when you were still asleep I heard the perfect song by the last cicada in the camphor tree. It is genuinely unique. After its singing, it changed into transparent wreckage. This happened at the last rhythmic sound. Wait a minute, you should say something."

"Me? I was thrown into the chamber pot as soon as I was born. Because I was steeped in urine, my eyeballs protrude, my neck is soft and weak, and my head was swollen like a ball when I grew up. I have breathed in poisonous air for half my life. My chest is eaten up by tubercle bacillus. My father is a syphilis patient, his nose rotted into two horrifying tiny holes. And my mother. . . . My home is on the ruins. There stands an empty old house, the only one in the area. I sleep inside with my family. During the day we search for scrap bronze and iron. Everyone refuses to give up and wears himself out. When night comes, we sneak in panic into the house like rats looking for the darkest and remotest place. I have longed to rest. Sometimes everything stops in the sun. I glare at a bunch of tiny pink flowers in the rubble, hoping my eyes can have a brief rest—my eyeballs are always swollen and pained. Why should all those flowers have pale faces?

"I remember that rainy morning when Father stepped in heavily from the outside in his overshoes, messing up the floor with rainwater. Then he came near me, telling me in a roundabout way that according to the lab experiment there were leeches in my lungs. While he was talking, his whole body twitched with restrained laughter. He believed that he had fulfilled a magnificent mission. When I walked out on my family, I couldn't straighten my legs. As a result, I fell flat repeatedly, plunging my body into the mud. As a matter of fact everybody knew about my walking out. This was an open secret. They only snorted through their noses, considering my unconventional actions despicable."

"Little flowers? Pale? I understand this completely." The old man lowered his head and mumbled confusedly. Suddenly his eyes brightened. He said energetically, "The crow is sitting on the darkened gravestone. At one caw, twelve years have passed. The grave is covered with sweet-scented roses. Two muddy feet tramp on the fine-leaved Chinese mosla. Even during the day there are spirits wandering about."

The mist was gradually retreating from us. In the distant, dark ruins, the burning sunset glowed scarlet. The gloomy silhouette of the old house was softened, green water dripped from the eaves. On the roof sat my father, who is suffering from an advanced stage of syphilis. He looked like a running sore. With him was my fat mother, dying of diabetes. The two supported each other, crushing many tiles under their weight. My brothers were crawling here and there like monkeys. In their transparent empty bellies huge stomachs were convulsing, greenish fluid oozing out. They were all staring at the smoky gray sky with their blank whitish eyes, making a clumsy gesture of expectation. Moving my lips, I was thinking of shouting something, but suddenly my vision was obscured by a vast haziness.

" 'Mother,' you are thinking of saying 'Mother,' " the old man said, pausing at each syllable. He appeared very weary. "I don't have much time left. These days I always see the rainbow. That happens during my stroll toward the graveyard. Sometimes even when I am asleep. It's a kind of familiar unexpectedness."

"Who are you?!" My hair stood on end.

"Me? The cremator." He put his hand on my shoulder. "I'd like to have a nap. Do you mind? It's so quiet here. I have chosen a place to lie down. There, under the clump of grapes, next to the little pool. Nobody has ever drunk the water there except black crows. Some people will come and lie with me, so I have dug many holes. One day they will come, a girl leading the way. They will kneel down to drink from the pool. Then they will fall into those holes on the fine-leaved mosla at the bottom. So, you have endured those long winter nights?"

"I have to rub my frostbitten toes constantly. I can't stop or I'll turn into an icicle."

"In the ice-sealed graveyard, red squirrels dance with their scarlet tails swinging on the snow-covered ground like burning candles, 'Ding ding dong, ding ding dong.' " Tapping the bark of the China fir with his finger, a mysterious smile hanging on his lips, he fell into sleep.

I leaned on the skylight the whole day, observing carefully the goings-on in the distant ruins. At the beginning I could see nothing but the mist. At noon the mist retreated little by little and the sun rose high, but at the old house it was dusk already. A column of thick smoke came out of the chimney and condensed in the sky, forming a motionless mushroom cloud. All of a sudden, the door of the cellar opened wide. My old aunt galloped out on the back of a mad bitch dog. They circled on the slag before dashing back into the cellar. The door banged in a painful sob. From somewhere a bell rang, numerous gray shadows of heads rose from the rubble, a green snake crawled between the shadows. The door was open again. Mother was pushed out in a bathtub. Her head was covered with blood. In one hand she held high a cluster of white hair with clumps of skin attached to the roots. She couldn't scream because her voice was blocked by a bone in her throat. The bathtub was so tall that she failed time and again in attempting to climb out. The old man moved, his eyelids released two drops of blood, and spasms of white foam poured from his lips. "I'm OK now." He sounded sorry while spitting out broken teeth behind me.

When darkness fell, the old man dug a hole in the piled-up mosla. We squeezed into the hole, then sealed the entrance. Uttering an uncomfortable sound, we fell asleep in a minute. Red dragonflies surrounded me, dancing and circling, tracing out countless rings of light. Everytime I was about to wake up, the rings swung me into deeper dreams. I was bending low to pick up a narcissus when someone pushed me hard from behind.

"Won't you go and see my grapes?" resounded the old man's voice, hoarse from a common cold.

We sneaked out of the hole like two old cats at night.

Again I felt the floating sensation under my feet. Amid the underground noise an alarm clock was ringing.

A gust of wind came, a bitter wind, chilling me to the bone in a way I had never before experienced.

I bent down and groaned, clutching my belly.

"The grapes are good." The old man stooped down. Making clicks, he grabbed my hand and stretched it toward the darkness. I touched a heap of something soft and wet that felt like the entrails of an animal. It had a sour stench. I jumped up, shrieking in terror.

"For starters"—the old man's hand was pitching and playing with the "grapes," putting them into his mouth continuously—"they move very slowly, but accelerate gradually. One winter night I saw those shadows frozen on the roof. And that was when I saw the rainbow for the first time, in a state of half-sleep. It happened so suddenly that I didn't fully realize. It has appeared again several times, and now I have gotten used to it. The hole I dug is right under us. You can feel it with your feet."

I probed with my toes, again touching those soft, wet entrails on which grew tiny, sucking disks that stuck to the blood vessels on my feet and refused to let go. Quickly I withdrew my feet and brushed the insteps with my hands.

"I often meet such a thing. While strolling among the gravestones, I raise my head to see a scarlet wine glass hanging in the sky, muddy yellow rice wine rolling and foaming, spilling from the rim. I listen and listen. It's all dead silence, only the evil froth bubbling and gurgling in the sky. Won't you try some grapes?"

He stretched sticky cold fingers to touch my hand. I shrank back, dodging here and there.

The carnivorous night bird was coming back, its two green eyes glaring covetously. With its wings tapping the branches, it sprang on me. I tried to dodge but bumped my head against something hard. Two pincers gripped my waist tightly.

"Say 'Please.' " In a daze I heard the old man's taunting voice.

"Please," the word slipped out of my mouth without my knowing what I was doing.

All over the ground were thick black branches. In the dim light from nowhere, I could vaguely see the old man's dark blue legs, soft and thin. They looked like intestines.

I spewed down from the sky everything in my stomach.

"The dance is very feverish." The old man sank into meditation. "That's my mother, who can never stand loneliness. Every night she will cimb up from underneath for the hunting. Her brain has already been emptied by the ants. Just listen: 'Pong-pong-pong, pong-pong-pong!' Like that, she will dance the whole night through. Astonishing sexual desire! She is a bit tough, isn't she? That's her all the time. I used to feel afraid, but now it's all right. I'm an indecisive man, and disgusting to others. I've been trying to learn from Mother, trying all my life, but in vain."

My heart still fluttered with fear when I recalled the two pincers and my body shivered with pain. The pupils of the night bird were still floating on the air. As if giving out some signal, they enlarged at one minute and shrank in the next. There was an illusory murderous smell in the air. I could feel it and was so discouraged that I couldn't raise my head.

"The creature is always after me. Do I smell of stale flesh? Here everything lives to the last minute. Since the shadows get frozen, I count my age as one hundred and three in my heart. I've dug so many pits and holes. Because of an innate shortcoming in temperament, I've been hesitating all the time, wearing deep grooves around the pits and holes, splashing loudly through the puddles. The sun at noon is shining in the Chinese photinia, casting a short, small shadow. Suddenly I see the pomegranate tree. The clock ticks its hands under the ground before it stops. Between the sky and the earth, there recurs the dead silence. In an instant, I have changed my mind."

"Who are you?"

"An old chap who digs tunnels in the graveyard. Here everything needs to live on until it becomes transparent remains that give a 'pong-pong' sound when you tap them. Just now you were about to pick a narcissus, a white cloud drifting above you, Chinese photinia surrounding you, a breeze blowing eternally. The alarm clock jingled. You will see a pomegranate tree growing on the red earth and the illusory flower blossoms filling the tree."

"My mother is sitting in the bathtub. Her scalp is peeling off." I was describing something new which grew out of my lungs like young sprouts and made my chest so full.

"Oh, Mo-ther." His tone was sarcastic.

"Cooking smoke is curling upward from the kitchen chimney. Inside the dusty screen window the fire in the fireplace is burning. My young brother is forty this year. I am three years older than he." My voice became clearer.

Again we squeezed into the straw cage.

We were swung into deep, deep dreams, far from each other.

Distant thunder was heard from the end of the forest. That was him snoring at the other side. There was no narcissus in the bushes. Under every tea bush there was a gray eyeball, which blinked constantly, giving out clear, dewlike tears. I picked up one of them, but immediately it turned into powder and a puff of smoke in my palm.

I remembered that I had come here in midsummer. My hat was on my head and my white shirt was bright and dazzling. I was looking for mushrooms with a bamboo basket in my hand.

I looked round and round. Sties grew in my eyes. In the ticking of the alarm clock, half of my life had passed.

With effort I opened my swollen and bloodshot eyes to the dead red dragonflies covering the ground. A wild cat was yowling bitterly in the bushes.

The thunder was coming nearer. The old man was lying under a ginkgo tree. His two feet had already become transparent. The man-eating night bird was perched on the branch holding back its eyelight. He was sunk in a deeper dream, which must have been purple because there was purple light above his head. There was no way for me to enter his dream. The grown-up sprouts were suffocating my lung.

The skylight appeared among the branches of the ginkgo like a black hole on top of the straw house. Midges swarmed out like thick smoke from the hole. Two men in gray came to the house and wrote on the wall with gypsum two huge letters: T X. Then they left, tramping on the Chinese mosla.

We woke up at dawn. From the distance came the remote bells: Ding-dong-dong. Three times altogether, it was so neat. So there was a clock in the old house and the man who rang the bell was none other than my father. The whole thing was farcical. Before I came here the clock was placed in the cellar, and it was covered with a thick layer of green mold. One fine day I tried to move it out into the sun, but only ended in dropping it on my feet.

They had really rung the bell three times. The ringer was my father. I could tell that from the bell.

"They have rung the bell," I said.

"I have just now heard the incomparable song of the cicada." The old man glanced at me attentively. He felt some kind of premonition. With a shaking hand he picked off the straw from his temple.

At the other side of the graveyard, the rainwater had filled the pit. Rotted grass was floating on the surface. Beside the pit squatted many toads.

"I can't cough. Inside something has just grown up. It may be bamboo shoots. I still haven't gotten used to it. . . ." I held my chest with folded hands as if I actually smelled burning pinewood.

"You also have seen the rainbow. I was standing by the lamppost observing you. Your eyes became two iceballs. The feeling is perfectly true. When the cold wind blows we are nothing but two dark shadows walking on the bare hill, with nothing to do with each other, walking in solitude."

"The ceiling is flashing with red light. A story remains in the ashes. I know how hard it is and I know that eternal dread." My throat throbbed with sharp pain.

"They would say 'Happy New Year!' " The old man held his laughter in his throat. At the same time, he held his sadness between his eyebrows.

"It's not important. You know this: a butterfly was flying in the forest; in the sunshine its wings shone like scarlet satin. She flew and flew for such a long time. At night I heard her falling to the ground with a crash, clear and pleasant. The starlight was dim, the trees were sobbing. In your dream your eyes dripped with blood."

"Happy New Year! Happy New Year!" The old man was mumbling. Climbing out of the hay, he stamped his deep footprint on the muddy path.

From the skylight, I could see far and wide. The old man was crouching in the early morning wind, tilting his stiff face against a rough gravestone. Surrounding him were holes he had dug several steps from each other. The sun reflected dazzling white light from the water, making a glass world of his surroundings. The frigid ground was full of cracks. A man was crawling up from the bushes at the end of the graveyard. Every now and then he stretched his long thin soft arms toward the sky and shouted some muffled sentences. That was my young brother. Within one night, he had grown a mole's tail and fur. In his

degenerated memory his image of me was vague. Slobbering, he tried to catch some yellow fantasy. Finally,
driven by certain elusive ideas, he crawled here from
the cellar. Mother was sitting on a barrel in the cellar,
mumbling an odd, unfamiliar name. She was in the
process of melting, a fine stream of black water ran
out under her feet toward the door. Father had started
ringing the bell again, with his hips sticking up in a
comical way: "Ding-dong-dong." Three times, three
somewhat scared strokes. As soon as he dropped the
iron hammer, one of his eyes went blind. The bamboo
shoots swelled in my chest.

The gray figures were gone long ago. The
writing on the wall had been washed away by the rain
at night. So it rained during the night. At the time I
was traveling in the midsummer sun.

It was so empty and still there. And there
was the wind.

In the sky there were false stars, drifting all
the time.

The fireplace was warm. Another story condensed in the gray mushroom-shaped smoke.

Many people walked down from the rubble,
and they went toward the old house along the cinder
road. Their backs looked longish and drifting. Their
steps were light and flightly. There were some other
houses in the ruin and some other people. Years ago
I had forgotten that.

The reddish street lamps were flashing. The
lampshades creaked in the cold mist. There was a layer
of silver frost on the ground. A lean man started whis-

tling, the reddish yellow flame dancing up from the window glass. Steam blurred the image. Many figures swayed on the moldy wall. The house was shaking and creaking. The icicles were falling from the eaves.

The old man was frozen into a transparent ice block. The night bird was asleep.

Long, long ago, I went with him to the forest to look for the mushrooms. He hadn't started digging holes then.

He took my betrayal too seriously and moved to the other side.

The night bird would be awakened when it rained. Flapping its wings, it would swallow his remains. The pits were full of water with dark, rotted grass on top.

Hurrying forward I had broken through the white light in the glass world.

"You want to put on a disguise?" The man in gray stopped me at the edge of the forest. He had no head but hummed his voice in his chest.

I heard the ding-dong behind me. That world was breaking apart.

"No, no, I only want to change my underwear and a pair of shoes. Then I will comb my hair. Very simple matters. If it's possible, I intend to take some butterfly samples, that red butterfly."

"In the winter night, I would listen to those footsteps carefully and straighten up the story about the Chinese parasol. It was dark outside, and it was dark in the room. My cold fingers touched the watch. I scratched several times before a shaking fire burned up. Many people floated out through the window, many, many. I could touch their flesh by stretching my hand. I bit their cheeks feeling delight in private. I would sit to the last moment in the dark night, smiling coldly, smiling tenderly, smiling bitterly. By that time, the old lamps would turn off and the bell resound."

At long last I was fascinated by my own voice. It was a kind of low voice, both soft and beautiful. It poured out eternally to my ears.

The

Instant

When

the

Cuckoo

Sings

I was lying in an old chair in the train station. The paint on the chair was fading. Some small insects were rattling under the chair. The air was full of smoke. Somebody farted loudly. Peering between the slats on the back of the chair, I could see many necks black with dirt.

"The wooden bridge was about to break. It shook with every step when I was walking on it. I became dizzy. . . ." the man sitting next to me was recounting in a melancholy tone, and there seemed to be no end to it once he started talking. A mouthful of big pink teeth was faintly visible in the blue smoke. His brown lips wriggled, opening and closing, causing his teeth to clash loudly. Two teeth were broken. Lips protruded as he swallowed his saliva.

I closed my eyes and tried hard to go back to the place. There was a playground. The eaves kept dripping day and night. The child had a clear white face which always had an irresistible enchantment to me. Many years ago he was a real person. When the sun shone into the classroom through the cracks of the roof tiles, he was sitting beside me in his blue shirt. On his chest he had pinned a specimen of butterfly with golden spots on its wings. His childish glances were soft and shy. Ever since that time my blood surged when I met his glance.

I stood up and felt my way out along the wall. I was determined to search for him on every street and every lane. The tiles on the roofs scraped sharply in the wind. It was midnight. I knocked open one closed door after another, only to find, to my terror, the reflection of light from the mirror inside with a big green caterpillar crawling across it. I moved my sweating toes. The floor shook violently under my feet. However, I know I will meet him soon when the cuckoo gently sings three times. On his chest, he will forever have that golden butterfly and his white teeth will shine.

Once when I met him I decided that I would see him again the next night at the same place. I ran all the way there out of breath, but his image had faded. His blue shirt turned gray and white, his hair had become rat-gray. A doctor came and hinted to me that I might be suffering from cancer. His face was hidden in a wicked smile. That night was a night of bad luck because somebody tried to dig out the foundation of the house and cut open the screen window to let in a cobra. The next day when I got up my ears were sore and swollen.

Once I saw him during the day. That was a noon with burning sun. I felt ashamed when I saw him. He was an out-and-out dwarf. His pale shanks were hairless. Like me, he was getting on in years. Without recognizing me, he sneaked away like a thief. I stood there for such a long time that the tar on the road melted into two holes under my feet.

Often, but unexpectedly, we met at night. That was in a pitch-dark house among many mirrors. His body was unusually warm, and I could hear the blood coursing through his veins. I suggested we play a game. Holding hands tightly, we walked into those mirrors. We beat down the green caterpillars and spat toward the outside. His childish smile forever held an irresistible charm for me.

"The train is due in at four," an old man said from the corner. He was coughing and spitting endlessly. I thought my lungs would fill my whole chest when I heard that noise; the pressure was so great that I wanted to vomit them out. Many dark shadows were twisting and turning against the wall. A baby fell to the ground with a muffled thump. "The cuckoo will sing at any minute," the old man told me. His eyes were like two dim oil lamps. "Whenever the cuckoo sings, I smell pine mushrooms. It has happened for seventy-three years. I've been observing you from this corner for a long time. You are waiting for the song, eh? I know a man who died of cancer. All the time he struggled not to go to sleep. He waited and waited; finally, he became exhausted. What you now feel is a tree, is my guess right? Every man has his own feeling. Some smell the water chestnut and some see Little Red Riding Hood. But I smell the pine mushroom. I am quite used to it. It is seventy-three years now."

Behind the house, a man was digging a spring. "Thump, thump. . . . " The sound lasted year in and year out. I have never seen that man. Every time I ran out of the house, he would flee without any trace. Only a hoe was left beside the hole, that and a rusty canteen. Something was wrong with the spot that he chose. There was no way to dig for water in that place. In my mind that man was a beggar and looked very much like me. I went to ask Mother. She said there was no spring at all. It must be my imagination. She also complained about my grumbling over hunger and searching for food everywhere in the house like a hungry dog. This is really outrageous!

One day while knocking at those closed doors, I suddenly realized that I was knocking at the wet brick wall. I felt my finger joints; they were broken and rotten. I turned to get out of the narrow lane, but I couldn't find the exit. I circled round and round and suddenly it came to me that I had fallen to the bottom of a well. That night the cuckoo didn't sing. In the morning I found my eyes clouded with cataracts. According to Mother, it was because of my weak constitution and the only therapy was to drink brain tonic constantly. I did it for two days until I could hardly raise my eyelids. On the third day he came.

My whole body was burning hot and my eyes were red as blood. We sat at our desk side by side. I accidentally overturned an ink bottle. He cleaned up the ink for me, smiling timidly. His childish lips were as red as roses and a swath of black hair was hanging right between his eyebrows. His eyes were fixed on the childish and innocent corners of my mouth and the red strings around my pigtails. I listened, holding my breath, for I knew that as soon as the bell rang outside, he would fade and wrinkles would crawl up to the corners of my eyes. I touched the burning hot desk and twisted in the chair painfully.

I said, "Tomorrow let's meet here again. Wait for me. We'll be able to see each other once we make

Dialogues

in

Paradise

Poetry accompanies

you forever,

Seducing you

to create

miracles.

One

an appointment. We've done that twice before. It's no good if we forget to make the next appointment before we go. Otherwise I might not be able to see you for a long time. One day I saw you in the street. I said to myself, 'That must be him. I know it as soon as I see him coming.' But it turned out to be a dwarf, and I thought it was you. I can never get it clear." The bell rang. His lips turned greenish gray. I dashed out of the classroom in a fury.

The old man followed me, saying, "It's not surprising. Everyone's the same. There are all kinds of images, sounds, odors occurring at the instant when the cuckoo sings. For instance, I can smell only the pine mushroom. I can prove. . . . "

I made up my mind to remain in that bright and beautiful instant. I sat under the husk tree feeling as empty as a robe. "Tap, tap, tap. . . ." Scarabs fell down like rain drops, all in red and green. I stretched my neck. My clothes were about to fly with the winds. I carved the word "HIM" on the bark with my dry, cracked nails. I raised my head and propellers as small as broad beans met my eyes on every side. A screaming cat dashed between my legs. It was always that shifty-eyed cat. While I was carving the word "HIM" I had a strange sensation as if the blue-shirted boy were sitting by my side. I had the same feeling sometimes in the dusk when I heard the digging of the spring behind the house and saw a bluish purple morning glory dancing in the darkness. Then the neck turned red and eyebrows curved into two bows. In the end, it was always that green-eyed black cat.

I once asked my mother why it was that at night all the closed doors would open at the first knock and then there was always the same horrible mirror? Mother said that was because I was suffering from pulmonary emphysema. All the patients with that disease would like to knock at someone else's doors. They could not reach a balance in their heart of hearts, and their whole lives were driven by the impulse for adventure. While she was talking, the inner part of her middle finger swung like a snake's head. Then she continued clearly, "I have seen your man."

I shrieked, digging the lime from the wall with my ten fingers until they were bleeding.

Before dawn, many living things bumped against the windowscreen and died. I went out of the room and heard a rustling of footsteps following me. "Venus is swimming up there, can it be a moth?" the voice of the old man squeaked out between his teeth. I turned my head and really saw him. He was only a rat. I remembered that in the past the old man was not a rat, but the rat by the wall could only be him. He was gazing at me, his beard shook and his eyes looked just like two oil lamps.

"The butterfly specimen . . . " I mumbled in confusion.

It was only the squeak of a rat, but I could hear the old man shouting, "Please look at that piece of red glass along the edge of the sky. Long, long ago, there were no dinosaurs or whales, but cuckoos had already been there. The bird sang, and then there

were the pine mushroom, butterflies, the Riding Hood!"

There was a hole near the drainage jumped into the hole, stretching his small looking head. He was still shouting.

The sun rose and my cataracts we pearing. I saw vaguely the man who was di spring—it was only a dead broken branch against the trunk in the wind. That was the dug so hard at dawn that he was sweating The thundering noise hurt my ears and rai boils there.

I understood once again I had lost t ment. I held the stove tightly and my who shrank into a vile skin-bag. Somebody got u bed. I could hear the sound of a toothbrush the tooth glass. Then a cool breeze blew swift the scent of wild chrysanthemum.

I know that tomorrow, or at a certai I will hear the song of the cuckoo again.

L ast night I smelled the fragrance of the tuberosa for the fifth time since you told me about it. When you first mentioned it, I pricked up my little ears, alert to a rushing sound: a ginkgo swaying in the deep water right at the center of the lake. The tree was full of tiny bells. When the bells sparkled, they jingled in splendor. I moved my left toe and heard the wind outside the door blowing away somebody's garbage can. It is always the goddamned south wind.

Just before its attack, I felt a strong, restless form growing inside me. I touched my legs and found them lithe and smooth like a snake. I sat up, stretching my long thin fingers, and grasped at the air. A vital ether flowed through my fingers. The fragrance was different from that of the ordinary tuberosa. Had I really concentrated, I would have realized it did not exist. With eyes wide open, I searched the darkness and finally noticed a line of tiny, perhaps illusory figures sneaking along the foot of the wall. Then my legs became soft and cold, drifting in the air like seaweed.

That first time I stood with you at a picturesque lakeside. My eyes became red and swollen, and I could no longer see anything. I shook, about to fall into the lake, when you held me up by my waist. "Tuberosa," you said. "Tu-be-ros-a!" Your face twisted in terror. You lowered your head, staring at your blood-red palms. It was then that you told me the secret of the tuberosa. You told me to wait for it every midnight. There would be a time when it would fail to come because it had never existed anywhere. You also told me in a seductive tone, like green, drifting sparks, "You can only wait."

Yesterday I indulged myself in the wild fantasy of waiting on that deserted hill at the back of my house. The sun was burning and I was sweating all over. My hair soon became wet and stiff. Someone discovered what I was doing and laughed at me, gestured excitedly, and even shot bamboo darts at my back, making hundreds of holes in my white overcoat. I waited the whole day in vain.

Tired and discouraged, I retreated to my hut, dragging my swollen legs. At midnight I tossed about and kicked away the quilt. I realized I was surrounded by the quivering live ether. The vibration was so queer all my joints came apart and my limbs drifted on the air. "A fish," I murmured bashfully, narrowing my eyes as if drunk. With some faint disturbance, the fragrance spread outward from the corner of the room.

Even at that first experience, the fragrance seemed familiar. It has remained in my memory of that foggy morning long, long ago. Four times afterward, the fragrance became stronger and more real. Last night it felt suffocating, and I fainted. When I came to, a burning red ring of light swung in the room. The corner of my mouth twitched, and my eyes were full of tears. You sat on a stone bench outside. I recognized your black silhouette at once. Stretching your arms wide, you yawned and whispered to yourself: "The tiny spirits have been in an uproar all night." You paced up and down outside, sighing deeply. Bathed in those light rings, my cheeks shone red, my hair was gleaming.

If only I had fallen into the lake that first time, I would have been able to find the tree. I would have become a fish swimming here and there in the dark water. But now I must wait. On these tranquil, sleepless nights, I put my ear to the wall and listen. I hate the south wind. It disturbs everything when it comes and only its howling remains behind. In still moments the bells jingle beautifully. Why did you grab my waist? I would rather have fallen and turned into that fish so I could find the tree in the water. I wish I could rest among the thick leaves. At dawn I would float to the surface and move my lips to you who are pacing anxiously, and sink to the bottom again because the rosy clouds would blind me.

"Close your eyes and count evenly to five. You may smell it," you taught me. I experimented with this the whole night until my head hummed miserably. Finally, in sorrow, I covered my head with the quilt.

I met you in the darkness. You were a lonely sleepwalker, sitting motionless on a stone. It happened I had set out to look for bees that night, and I recognized you immediately. I couldn't wait to tell you that I had a huge hole in my chest with wet petals rustling inside. I also told you how I had feared cold since I was young. Rattling on, I put my icy fingers into your warm hands.

"The beehive is under that stone. I've been observing them night after night," you said. "You've come from the seashore. I heard you crossing the beach. The sand is fine and the wind is chilly. Your hair smells of the sea. The sea is far away. It has taken you more than a dozen years to reach me, and I've been waiting for you here all that time." You pressed my fingers to your cheeks and said, "It's OK now. As a child I also feared the cold very much. Now I've gotten used to it. Even on a snowy night I watch here alone because I'm not sure when you will appear. I was frightened that you might pass me by, leaving me here alone." That night we paced up and down, wearing a groove in the stony path.

I meant to ask how you survived. The place was so arid. The ground was covered with poisonous snails that would find their way in to bite you even though you closed the windows. You must have been thin and weak when you were young. Did you cry with your shoulders hunched when the cold wind blew and the Chinese parasol leaves hit the tiles? How could you wait so long in the same place without your feet being bitten by the ice and snow? Early when I was at the seaside, I saw a man wandering alone, breaking cobbles with his hands. Could it have been you? At that time I couldn't see clearly. In my memory there is also a cock. It crowed only on foggy mornings. Its crow was very loud. Have you ever heard it? However, I didn't ask you all these questions. I was afraid my voice would disturb the live air flow around us. It was passing through our clinging arms softly and smoothly.

The next morning of our meeting, we took off our shoes and romped on the stony path barefoot. We laughed and trampled numerous small poison snakes. In each buttonhole, we put a honeysuckle blossom. I no longer felt fearful because you were holding my hands. Your steps were so steady. Later on you grew into a strong man. The sun was hot in the sky, but we were still romping, faces red and bright. We shouted to each other, "*You* are the person."

At the seashore once, I thought I would never find you. I cried and buried myself in the sand, waiting for the quiet end of life. Lying there, I was tired and sad. Watching the dark shadows overhead, I was frustrated. Yet I listened. I could not stop. It had become an instinct. Your voice woke me. I climbed out of the sand and ran like a gust of wind in the direction of your call.

I should tell you something else important. When I would wait for the tuberosa at night, a dark shadow stood at the door. When I shut my eyes, he moved toward me. I shivered and dared not sleep. One day when I couldn't help dozing off, his long arm stretched out and snatched my hair. I was horrified. I screamed for you until my throat swelled red and my tongue was dry and tired. I didn't understand how he had come in; I checked all the windows and doors in fear every night before going to bed. Sometimes he could not come in — when you were sitting outside my door. My heart was at ease when I saw your dark silhouette. I usually slept peacefully. Can you appear on that stone for a time every night? I am so very terrified.

Maybe I really will become a fish. Then you won't be able to see me. At the lakeside early in the morning you will see only a fine, tiny fish jump from the water and move its lips to you and disappear. Then your heart will be torn to pieces and your head will spin like a windmill. I have no heart to change into a fish. I will search for the tuberosa with you in the dark, you outside, I inside.

Two

This place is severely drought-stricken. There is only a deep, nearly dried-up well whose water is all muddy. The green is disappearing from the earth, leaving sun-dappled lizards crawling everywhere. The roads are cracking. Dreams are long and sere, full of the smell of dust. Every night I come out to look for bees. One dark, windy night, you sped past me in quick, short steps, wrapped in a shawl. I recognized you at once, and you me. Your shoulders shivered almost unnoticeably. Stopping, you fixed your eyes on the pitch-dark road and said, "How lonely and dull the night is. Listen, the glacier is breaking up."

The wind was howling between us. The moon was only a lightless shadow. I strained to hear your breath in the wind.

"In the past, I knew you very well," you whispered, shaking in the wind. "There was a shining crystal ball on your windowsill and a huge black umbrella hanging from the ceiling. Sometimes you glanced at the window glass by chance and saw a pale, beardless face, smooth and meaningless. I used to live in the hut under the mulberry tree. On the nights when the stars were gleaming, there was always a lion roaring in the distance. I groped my way outside. The ground was like a furry animal skin. I saw my heart shrink into a lump of dried lemon."

I was silent. I wished I could tell you about that pasture. The wind was very hot, the sky very blue, flying wasps filled the sky and people were running on the grass. The planes in the distance looked like tiny beetles . . . I didn't say this. What I spoke about was the well: "The well is drying up gradually. When I was young, I cried sitting by the well before dawn. The nightingale would sing sadly somewhere. At dawn people lined up to pour stones into the well. It's a long, long story. I felt cold. Later, I started to pay attention to my appearance. I hung strings of grapes around my neck, one string and then another. In the darkened room I waited anxiously for a landslide. I cut a hole in the roof with a pair of scissors. Stretching my frenzied head through the opening, I thought I heard a rumble in the distance. You must surely be losing your patience listening to this story. There might be someone on the highway. I always remember this when I am wandering around here. Sometimes those tall electric poles change into human beings."

In the distance regular, mechanical footsteps sounded on the highway. I clung to you. The earth undulated under our feet, charming and dissolute. My heart collided with yours. We seemed relieved. Your breath was soft, as fine as a hair. "My skin is a special crystal," you whispered in my ear. "There are countless small red fruits in the southern forest, and wild animals hide in the bushes."

I felt more and more anxious to talk about the pasture, the hot wind. But once my mouth was open, I spoke about the man on the road again. I could hear your eyelashes flicker. My face turned red with shame.

"It's only the icy drops on your lashes," you patted my cheek calmly as if you were coaxing a child. "It is too cold. That man does not exist. You would need only to shut your eyes quietly, and we would appear under the ginkgo tree. Up above, a sea of stars is rolling like waves. Don't be impatient, gently, gently, one day maybe we will have a try."

You are always like that. That's why I can recognize you at once, no matter where. I recognized you when I had the grape string on my chest. You were small. You stood at the road sign observing me, your dark eyes unusually serious. I tried talking about something, but you turned and walked away. You never came back after that. But I knew that once you appeared I would recognize you. I have stayed here fighting the drought. My chapped soles are bleeding. My temples are burnt yellow. I can't remember how I survived those dusks. Whenever the branches of the Chinese scholar tree would crack, I cut a hole in my roof letting in a flood of light. Now my roof is practically a sieve.

Yesterday somebody stole my hoe. I used it to open up the wasteland. I planted something every now and then, but nothing survived because there was no rain. All afternoon, I sat dully listening to that man digging as if he were showing me how. Here no stars appear at night. All we have is an artificial moon like a paper cutting. My eyes have long since gotten used to observing things in darkness. I sat on the stone motionlessly. When you turned around that hill, I heard your footsteps. I shivered at that time, saying,

"A man." Sitting on the stone, I felt as ancient as this savage place. Maybe I have lived too long? From I don't know when, life has been stretching in one direction, infinitely, empty and dull, with no obvious mark to separate it into stages. I tried to flow away from this body, but it only resulted in my eyes turning a strange color. Now they can no longer distinguish day from night. I pretended to go out to find bees, but I knew it was ridiculous. "Hold me tight, hold me tight. Look at that huge python. Your toe is on the pulse of the earth."

"Oh, I don't care. Why should I care! I used to jump here and there in the forest without anything on. It's really cold at night here. How can you live for so long? Have you always been like that? Did you really cry when you were young?" You bombarded me with questions, blowing puffs of warm air, stamping your small feet, and walking in a circle. You put a shivering, pale, slim palm on my chest. "Is the burning sun so severe during the day?"

You told me you were from a place with starlight. Your hut was under a mulberry tree. Standing under the tree, you could see the sunset glowing like fire. You walked out long, long ago. The jackdaw built two nests on the dead branch.

"The mud-rock flow dashed down the mountain ferociously. One day, I arrived at a grayish white graveyard. I sat the whole day." You finished your story. Ice-cold tears covered your face.

"Hold me. Hold me tight. Its teeth are about to bite your ankle. You have stepped on the pulse of the earth. In the wind, there might stand a man . . . "

"But you said it was nothing but a pole. Wait, wait, ah, I think I have heard the roaring wave of the stars."

The wind was blowing from the mountain. It had the foul smell of dried animal skin. On a fine day we were dozing off warmed by the sun amid a bunch of wild chrysanthemum blossoms, idly watching the passing wild geese. I often thought I had already forgotten this.

"Lately, I search everywhere. I was standing there, the broken shadow of dried branches swaying before my eyes. It dawned on me that nothing at all could be found. Holding my empty head, I squatted down pondering something. My story is both long and dull. Listen, the ground is frozen. Let's have another look; there might be one nightingale left, a tiny creature which hasn't yet flown away."

I planted garden burnet, fernleaf hedge grass, and roses. It was drizzling at the time. On my way back, I always met that man on the muddy path. He had a cone-shaped bamboo hat and kept his head low. I couldn't see his eyes. We passed each other in a hurry. I always felt I had lost something. This situation lasted several years. Then it stopped raining. Because of the wind, the ground was covered with dust all year round. I still met him. He was by the pole at the roadside. He wasn't wearing his bamboo hat. But still I couldn't see his face, which was vague and unclear. He appeared there, so we passed each other, and again I had the feeling of loss, which now is rarer and rarer. Maybe the day will come when I won't recognize him at all.

You were still thinking of that. You said, "If we go straight ahead holding hands with our eyes shut, we might reach the hut under the mulberry. Sometimes the small zigzag path disappears in a stretch of purple desert. I have long forgotten the place. Touch my hair, you will find it as stiff as a horsetail. This is the result of the combing of the cold wind. The window of your house is wide open all year round. You won't give up. You hate to miss the shadows on the road. Whenever the shadow of a tree or butterfly sways before your eyes, you pace and sigh. You knock on the wall until it makes a hollow sound. When the white knotweed flowers blossom on the snow-covered ground, I stop before your window. We smile. Your eyes reflect two golden suns, and my mustache is also dyed golden. We only need to be more patient. There may be a day when we will have a try." That man appeared at the pole again — a narrow, long, dark shadow. I gazed at him, seized by hatred and fear.

"Quiet, quiet!" Your voice turned into a quick whisper. "Look at the flatfish in the star waves. The sun rises with the moon. The enchanting earth is twisting at her waist . . . quietly, under the ancient tree, the young head exquisite and beautiful!"

Three

I went out again last night. You had warned me not to wander around at night so as to avoid unexpected harm. I remembered your warning, but I went out anyway as if sent by a ghost or a god. I drifted down the staircase merely by raising my legs. Before me was a vast expanse of whiteness. I passed rows of tall buildings, went through rustling woods, walked by ancient rocks. All of these gave out an indifferent, colorless light. They were like a certain ruin lost track of in memory, both ancient and illusory. A grayish white night bird flew by my side. I know it was not a bird, but a paper crane I made in the kitchen long, long ago. It will accompany me till my last day.

I have been good at flying ever since I was young. This is my personal secret. Whenever something terrible chases me, I stand up lightly on my tiptoes and find myself on the lamppost. I kiss the ridges of the roof, scared as well as proud. It is easy to change direction and turn a corner. All I need do is raise or lower an arm. I am nimble and skillful and have never been caught, not once! However, there was something wrong last night. Soon after I left home, it started to drizzle. Though the sky was still white, my eyesight was all the more blurred. The damned cold must have caused this. I caught an old branch, stopping myself for breath. I thought of you.

That day I was lying in your bosom, stroking your hair and face, sighing. Suddenly I saw you hiding in the distant woods. As a matter of fact, what I recognized was nothing but a huge color picture, a stereoscopic picture. You faded in and out and could also move about. You hid first behind one tree then another. Your face kept changing, too. One minute you were my uncle, and the next minute you became my cousin. Then you changed back into your hazy self. It is said that people have invented a kind of photo which has the effect of a video recording. I overheard this one day in some lost empty house, and I can never rid myself of the impression. Maybe this is that kind of picture? I was opening my mouth to tell you who was holding me and what I saw, when I realized you were nowhere about. I was only playing a game with myself on the grass! But the color photo was real. When the fallen autumn leaves were rattling, you sat on a tall pile of logs, resting your chin on your hand. That day I bumped my head into the wall with an explosive sound.

I made up my mind once to find my uncle in order to clarify the whole thing: was there this kind of photo in this world? Why had I seen it ever since the beginning of my conscious life? I wanted to tell him what a great riddle it was and that I got the correct answer whenever I saw it. And that it became a riddle again when it disappeared and I completely forgot the answer. The problem was that it wouldn't come just anytime you wanted, but only when you had lost it from memory. And the figure in the photo was not always someone you wanted or expected; and his appearing would have nothing to do with any present anxiety. He would come without being summoned. So I asked my uncle, because I couldn't verify what I saw.

I rattled on with some incoherent nonsense, decorating it with numerous irrelevant metaphors intended only to surprise him. That was all.

Wretched drizzle. It was so cold. I dared not try the journey home like this lest the rainy weather cause me to lose my footing. Everytime you kissed my lips involuntarily, I would say, "My darling." At this you turned pale and cold immediately. Then you looked around, trying to avoid illusory wasps. So I became cautious and stopped saying "My darling." I held the expression in my throat, and combed your hair with my fingers in silence. But this didn't make much difference because you were sensitive, and you knew where I kept the phrase. You remained pale and quivering, your expression frozen like a mask.

Without making a sound, you said, "My left leg is suffering atrophy. You've mistaken me for the man who was throwing pebbles by the riverside one dusk. You've made such mistakes at least twice in your life."

You hinted that I shouldn't believe I could fly everywhere, penetrating everything. I couldn't. Take you, for example. You were a much greater riddle than the photo. Even now your existence remains a question. I shouldn't be so confident about your existence because you might disappear one morning in the stream of people and become one of the thousands of unfamiliar faces. You might not leave me, but I could have walked away when I recognized you were not the man throwing pebbles at dusk. When I realize my extreme frivolousness, I laugh idiotically.

The rain didn't seem likely to stop. I remembered a stone pagoda outside the woods where I could rest. I hunched over and raised my arms out level for takeoff. Although my flight was bumpy, I didn't panic. Generally speaking, my flying was OK, just as once I kept cool when a leopard chased me. I am always cool.

After I left the woods I realized there was no pagoda: it was not in the woods but riding the sea waves. It had a green light on top. I saw it when I was ten and could never forget it my whole life, just as I could not forget those color photos.

My first color photo appeared on the bedside cupboard when I was eight. The background in the photo was a yellowish green lawn. A boy in sky-blue embroidered shorts was playing football in the middleground. When I pushed the photo, he would wink his eye and kick the ball high. I was fascinated.

Circling round and round the open ground, I saw many tiny creatures wandering about down below. Among them were boars and leopards. I glided up and down and dared not land abruptly. I even recognized the rock on which you and I once lay. From above, it looked to be a dark round spot like gangrene on a gray-white body.

Your hand was warm and soft. I felt it while lying on the rock. The sun dyed your mustache brownish red. Your heaving, rolling, and tossing made several cracks in the rock. Countless birds flew up in panic.

When I told you my feeling, you were so startled you picked up a cobblestone and dashed it into pieces. "Nothing exists any longer." Raising your arm, you drew a big, irregular curve. Transparent butterflies drifted by lazily from behind you, one after another.

"I can fly." I gathered courage to argue. "Your hand is *indeed* beautiful. I cried when I was folding the paper crane."

You winked in a mysterious way: "The same. Many artificial things have proved our nonexistence. We are nothing but those elusive butterflies. In the moment when you feel my palm, it might be someone else's palm, and this someone else has already disappeared in the crowd. The sensation remains on your cheeks for a long time, but the whole thing is irrelevant to him. You might try to find him, but nothing can be decided. Sometimes he is throwing pebbles by the riverbank at dusk; sometimes he appears on top of the pagoda; and sometimes he is spreading a net in front of a ship. Every time he is a different person. You have to imprint your image of a quivering heart on one body after another. Every time it is real and vivid. These people provide flesh and blood and charm to this model. They make it enchanting and overwhelming. It will forever keep its youth, but you. . . ."

"Why should you kiss me?" You didn't answer my question. Your elegant fingers turned into something like rubber bands in my palm. I clenched my fist; an angry, throbbing blood vessel broke and blood oozed out gently, crawling down my arm like a red leech.

"When I was fifteen I broke my leg. Lying in bed I folded thousands of paper cranes. One morning I stretched my thin, greenish neck out the window. A frosty wind chilled me to the bone. Under the window the crowd bustled to and fro. I stayed there until dark, stuck to the windowsill by ice and frost. That time I almost lost my arm. I still remember the beautiful colors of those paper cranes, imaginary colors, delicate and tasteful. Finally the day came when a young man similar to you walked into my room and saw the cranes scattered on the floor. He was silent for a long time, then he stooped down as if about to pick up the little things. Quickly I flattened the one he intended to pick up. Our eyes collided in an explosion of little stars. I noticed a scar on his temple. He was the man. I knew this scarred face. I am talking about your past experience. We have met many times before. I used to be the crane-folding girl. You can't recognize this, of course."

The rain stopped, and I was ready to fly back. In the elusive empty house, on the gangrene-looking rock, I will meet you unexpectedly again. You will kiss my lips involuntarily. But I, next time, will say, "You are *he*, and I am the woman, by the river, at the lighthouse, in the front of the boat, on the beach under the burning sun at noon, in the sweet-scented osmanthus forest. In the warm drizzle of the south the buds of the red roses are about to blossom. A snow-white figure is standing still in the gray rain and frost."

Four

You enticed me to play the game the second time you met me.

"You will gain an unbelievable happiness."

The glittering cold spark from your eyes when you were saying this reminded me of the crystal you placed on your windowsill one dark night. It always flashed, giving out an enchanting, cold flame, aggressive and overwhelming. Instinctively, I retreated to the corner, my back to the wall. Digging at the wall with my fingers behind my back, I gave out a queer chuckle, pretending to be calm. With the chuckle as my weapon, I put on an air of indifference, glancing left and right. The flame extinguished, your eyes became two pieces of flat yellow glass, turbid and dusky.

"I can't be wrong." You stamped your foot impatiently and stubbornly before you dashed out. The empty room resounded with your steps. The floor cracked. My finger peeled down a big lump of lime.

I have passed through many cities. There are many people in the cities. Their eyes are all flat yellow glass, their hands cold and stiff, those people. All city people hustle and bustle, like a multitude of fish. Every night I hide in the woods, howling to the sky like a wolf. I've lost you and I have to pass through many more cities. With a false hope, I walk and walk.

Then the deep sleep; the cold flame burns again, its brilliant spark penetrating the vital organs of my body. The spark belongs to me in reality, yet

I recognized it in your eyes. Maybe we have the same type of eyes. Maybe the spark from one's eyes can light those of the other, though our own soul is always in chaos. We can only recognize ourselves in each other's eyes. In the deadly, sleeping, empty city prowls a wolf. In the blue sky hangs a lonely golden hook.

Finally, I play the game in imagination. Shoulder to shoulder we sit on the cliff, dangling our legs over the edge, kicking the rock. You are so calm I suspect this isn't your first time at the game. Hatred grows in my heart. The ghostly will-o'-the-wisps drift and wander in the empty valley. From the bushes rise ambiguous whisperings.

"We only need to leap off and we will gain a new soul. It is not at all difficult." You are seducing me. I can hear that your voice isn't reliable.

"Then I'll lose you." I finish your sentence without hesitation, feeling my body melt into the rock. The game simply can't start, even in fantasy.

I'd rather imagine. That makes my eyes retain the enchanting burning flame. (You've always told me that.) But my spark can't light my whole self. My soul is forever in darkness. I have to search, search the eyes that will light the darkness from the numerous yellow glasses. But once I find it, I will face the horrifying abyss.

You weren't wrong. It was I who pretended you were wrong. I remember once frowning and saying to you coldly, "Everything is in a mess." But at the same time, I broke two nails digging at the wall behind me. So many years have passed. The tree used to grow purple mulberries. Who can forget that? That stretch of dark fertile land, lascivious plant roots tied together, vigorous and dense, shapeless ghosts and goblins haunting them. That day, the spark from your eyes swept over it. Do you know what happened? Do you know what happened?

I have been searching. I may find something again. (This is a vast world.) It is an unbreakable wicked circle. Evil spirits rise in the profound darkness, hairy plants swell rapidly. Does the wolf in the iron cage run day and night in its narrow world? There may be a day when I decide to taste the happiness of a whole body of broken bones.

Waking up in the morning, I go out and see many, many people walking past me. I stare at those unfamiliar faces. I say in a loud affected voice, "Among you there must be one that I know." I stand there until night as if annoyed with someone. All the people walk past. They are only passersby in greasy overcoats. I often spend my days like this. You came in abruptly. I was playing with an hourglass when I heard the scrape of footsteps behind me. My eyebrows twitched. "Look at me," you demanded.

I didn't intend to turn around at all. As I gazed at the sand, the glass timer reflected my gloomy bluish face. You knew very well that I had observed your own reflection there and that it was not necessary to turn my head.

But you didn't give up; you repeated the same command, *"Look at me."*

That day I didn't turn my head once. You disappeared in the empty sky as abruptly as you had come.

"But the mulberry is such a remote hallucination!" I sighed, my feet unsteady.

Riding on a speeding train, I am going through an endless tunnel for thousands of miles. Your voice vibrates metallically in the tunnel, *"Look at me!"* A young man sits opposite me, wondering how I can stare at the plain window glass forever. He has a chin like yours, so I can't help turning around and smiling sadly at him, saying, "See, I've lost it. It's ridiculous. Somewhere the crawling vine grows like bacillus. . . . Maybe he's right. Why should I run like crazy? There is no escape."

I've left the hourglass in that house. This seems something with which to entertain dark schemes, and to play the coquette skillfully. All the way I've been reassuring myself that I am open and aboveboard, again and again. I try to cheer myself up. Deep in thought, I imagine you sitting at the table playing with the little thing. The glass reflects your pale face, filled with grief and indignation. A vicious sneer surges over your mouth. In the glass, you can observe me clearly. But I can see only your back and that pair of familiar hands. They are brimming with vigor and vitality!

"You can only come back. There is no escape. This is completely clear." Frowning, you groan. Some wound shoots bitter pain through your spine. Of course, the game is extremely simple. The cliff is trembling, the ghostly will-o'-the-wisps are wandering and drifting in the empty valley.

A woman follows me everywhere, a disheveled-haired, boisterous savage, laughing like a madwoman every now and then. Because of her, I dare not turn my head; my eyes remain fixed on the rosy clouds above the horizon. One stormy day, I hid from the rain in a run-down pavilion. My heart quivered. Turning around I saw her stop about ten feet away. Soaking wet, she was talking to me: "Then what? You can't verify anything. I've seen so many people with sparkling eyes. All of them are ugly and blind. They run to the field to swallow grass roots at night. They can't help themselves. What can you do?"

"Treasure. . . . " I spoke the word haltingly before she interrupted.

"Listen, poisonous snake, and wolf, I know how they threaten you in a certain place. Ferocious plants roar in the black wind. It's hard for you indeed."

Every time I reach a city, I presume you are waiting for me at the road sign. I memorized those road signs a decade ago. I loved to stop by them, staring at them, kicking the mud with my feet and circling slowly. Those ancient road signs always give me a cozy illusion. But you have never appeared. It is nothing but a one-sided game, utterly silly. Your glance was firm: you should stay where you are. You are as conceited as that, refusing to move a step even in destruction. Yesterday, one of your city folk told me you planted some trees at your door and have been watering them regularly.

"What's the matter with your eyes, photo-phobia?" he asked.

"Oh, yes, I'm going blind. So many double images."

It's possible that I will visit the ends of the earth (sometimes by foot, sometimes by train in the tunnels). Yet you will always remain there, sitting at the table sad but firm, glaring at the woman's image. Time flies, but you are forever young. Now I realize that it is I who am uncertain. I will flee in panic for-ever. Even if one day I clarify the doubt, I'll still be in fatal contradiction. You predict that I will return in spring. That day, you will rise from the table and open the door, only to find a white-haired woman. . . .

"What a wonderful instant! The tiny flowers in the dusk are full of tender thoughts, patches of purple-blue mist floating in the shady forest. Calming our stormy hearts, we run into the woods. The whole mountain resounds with the song of the oriole."

Sitting by the window, I love to rave like a lunatic. The only path has been blocked by the wild bushes. Who can forget that? I saw this horrible scene by the road sign. The talk about the mulberry is only fabrication. It's only by constant recollection that il-lusion turns into truth. I thought this way; I am think-ing this way.

"Wait for me, wait for me. . . ." I whisper in the rain.

Five

When I left you that day, I forgot to tell you what had happened during the night. Turning my head while running away, I saw you kick the huge rock off the cliff. The empty valley reverberated with its rumble.

After midnight every day all kinds of noises start in the house; queer voices speak in everchanging pitches resembling the waves in the sea. A shadow waves its hands energetically as if attempting to stop something in the middle of the room. It always starts roaring at a specific moment, a vague threat, lasting until about three. Its thundering voice quiets the room, and the air becomes thinner. If a lamp is turned on, one can see stifled mayflies dropping to the floor in spasms, their wings turning pink. I suppose it is a black cat as big as a leopard, blind in both eyes. Ferocious and wild. At the seashore, I hinted to you about the cat, but you smiled and said to the sky, "Everything has its reason to exist."

It leaves as soon as the cock crows. Immediately, I feel the heaviness of the pillow. I sit up and beat it forcefully, making a series of explosions. Those mayflies! Sometimes the cat departs earlier. And I am left at a certain gray highland. The rocks are cold, the sky is low, there are black, round holes in the ground. I feel them with the bottoms of my feet only to realize that they are not holes, but shadows. What shadows can they be? Looking around I can't see anything casting these shadows. There are only protruding rocks which can't possibly have round shadows.

"O, hey! O! O! O!" I shout your name on the highland, cold sweat running down my body. Shouting, I feel I should go ahead regardless of everything. Strangely enough, this doesn't lead to a sense of reality. I remain vague and broken. It would be more horrifying if I didn't shout. The black holes split, multiplying until the whole highland becomes a honeycomb. I don't even have a place to stand. Though I know the holes are only shadows, I dare not step on them. The shadows are unusual — shadows without objects. They might be traps.

I have to call you continually. That's why my throat is sore every morning, and I have to keep silent the whole day. I have to protect my throat, prevent it from bleeding at night, which has happened twice. It was miserable. A mouthful of blood poured out, staining my whole body. My mind summoned me back, yet my body was still left on the cold highland. Raising my head, I saw dim red stars. "O, O, O . . ." I could only whisper, waiting for the cockcrow, my salvation. But, in a swoon, I always missed the moment of the crowing.

I don't detest the cat. On the contrary, I'm expecting it every night. But it leaves me always at the same place. The situation occurs more and more. Despite my attempt to stop it, it disappears like magic, and I find myself standing on the deserted highland. That is to say, I have to control my fantasy and let matters slide. I keep my eyes open in the darkness. One smell of the air, and I know where it has reached. It always starts by scratching at the window frame with

one of its paws, then gives two short, sad cries. Next
it rolls on the ground, roaring. At the vague roar, I
am changed into a white whale swimming away from
my quilt. I swim around swinging my body in the air,
my tail tapping the wall. The whole room jingles. I
love to drift in the pure, empty sky, a stream of
thoughts surging forth.

We passed hand in hand through the woods.
The wind greeted us from no discernible direction. It
blew me off balance. But your pace was always steady,
your eyes narrowed, fixed on the white light in front
of us.

"There is something . . . " my voice trembled.

You held my fingers tightly, hinting at me to
stop.

The white light brightened your forehead.

The escape was unexpected and sudden. As
a result I didn't even have time to tell you anything —
who I was; where I was from; what plants grew on the
bank of the river I walked past; why I dried up in
spring and fall; why I collected leaves and searched
for the stifled mayflies at night, their wings being pink.
There were winds without direction in spring and fall.
It was in the wind that I found you. You were standing
under a tree, silent. Your young forehead beamed with
joy. The wind was ruffling the sand behind you. Taking a step, I staggered.

"Have you ever been to the river bank at the
flooding season . . .? " I chattered on hastily, raising
my hand to keep the blowing sand out of my eyes.

You remained silent, but looked at me again and again. Raindrops fell from the leaves, soaking our hair. Finally, you sighed, "I know you. You are just like this."

I had so many things to tell you. When I was talking you looked at me quietly, never interrupting. The air became so pure it looked bluish, a gloomy light blue. We always met at the same place, where fresh, cold raindrops fell from the leaves, even on a sunny day. Where were these raindrops from?

The stories were not what I wanted to say. I couldn't make myself clear, no matter how I tried. I remember I talked drowsily about the forest, the thatched shack, the footsteps in the dark room. I also complained about the honeycomb under the rock. God knows what rubbish I spoke. I always rattle like this, making a great mess out of something simple, and I regret afterward. At sunset, I sat at the door, holding light in my hands, my head hanging low. You were standing in front of me. Your limpid eyes told me you understood every word. I recovered my courage and tried again. Maybe I could give an account of what I wanted to say . . . But why should escape be necessary?

Long ago I didn't know there was a piece of highland somewhere which could be so ghostly at night. I never thought about things like this. Instead, I lay under the willow near the river sunbathing. In the flood season I would look across the river into the distance, expecting something.

"Don't stare at the sun. Don't concentrate your gaze too much," a voice kept whispering in my ear. "There is a fellow sitting on the swing."

The sunlight in spring and fall had a touch of decadence. The turbulent river was rife with the odor of reproduction, tree roots rotting in the water producing endless bubbles.

You and I stretched forth our hands, watching the raindrops dripping onto our palms, lost in counting, "One, two, three, four, five . . . "

"Someone is catching snakes there . . . " I started to say. I am decreed by fate to talk endlessly, maybe because I raised rabbits when I was young, living under the big mountains. It is foolish that my eyes cross when I talk too much, yet I have lost control. Every time you came I would talk. I was born with a fervent spirit. They say this was caused by the burning of the sun. I used to shout and run barefoot on the blistering beach. Raindrops gathered into a shiny pool in our cupped hands and a rhomboid, artificial eye appeared in each palm. "Fifty-three, fifty-four, fifty-five . . . " You were still counting silently.

"There are all kinds of highlands," you finally told me yesterday. "It's not necessary to run away. Just stay where you are, and your body will become translucent and shining. I've undergone all of this. Just keep calm. On the shady path, the rain drips all the time. I can hear raindrops wherever I go. I've never bathed in the sun. We lived in the caves on the big mountain. Just imagine the life. Every day I looked into the distance at the riverbank you passed. It is so clear in my mind's eye. While you were lying under the willow tree, I saw you trying to fly. It was a failure and you broke your leg. For many years, I could recognize you by your crippled form. Our meeting was predestined. Neither of us has sought the other. And these raindrops accompanying us are recounting some kind of eternity."

Your hut is at the other end of the deserted land, looking like a black, poisonous mushroom emerging from the ground at night. You never use the light, neither do you close the door. You're suffering from eternal insomnia. You count the hours, sitting on a chair, and never sleep deeply. When I rush in, your voice always greets me from a corner of the room: "It's great. I've driven away the leopards. They tried to ambush you on your way here, a big cat and two small ones."

Tonight I'll go to the deserted land with you. I've made two kites. We are going to shout and scream as we did in our childhood. You'll tell me, "Look there, look there, see how the wasps dance madly." We will fool around the whole night, forgetting our miserable sleeplessness, forgetting the dark city. Bending low, we will hear the voice of the earthworms. In the red sunlight, we will become two stalks of verbena with a chain of raindrops on our stems.

Afterword

Can Xue's

"Attacks

of

Madness"

by

Ronald R. Janssen

Better discuss the truth in dreams than what is false in so-called true statements.

Lu Xun, *Selected Works*

The stories of Can Xue contribute a vigor to our notions of fiction not unlike that derived a decade or so ago from the Latin American writers. Western readers can best appreciate the significance of her work by scanning the available anthologies of post-Maoist short stories, presentations of Chinese fiction that, with exceptions and once our initial curiosity is satisfied, are likely to seem narrow and unimaginative, a trudge through a desert posted with signs of "Realism" and "Socialist Realism," "New Realism" and "Critical Realism." It is no belittlement of the efforts of the earlier post-Maoist writers to say that their work reveals, over and over, a literature that had not yet, despite particular achievements, invented the forms that would enable it to rejuvenate itself. And it is not unfair to say that this general failure of aesthetic intuition was another of the legacies of Chairman Mao, who in his famous "Talks at Yan'an" (1942) sundered Chinese fiction from its own artfulness and bound it with such heavy ropes of prescription that, in an age bidding it to run, it could scarcely walk.

Can Xue's response springs from her temperament; all of her stories are born of unspecified miseries, of "attacks of madness" and "an impulse to 'break out' of desperation."[1] Like many of her characters, confined by circumstances, she would fly: "I often fly in my dreams, and every time there is something horrible

chasing me. I know I can't escape, yet I keep trying."
The "something horrible," we can guess on the evi-
dence of the stories, is authority, whether familial,
social, cultural — or literary:

> I can't deal with realism, and may not even in
> the future. I have to enter a kind of supernatural
> state to write anything creative. I have to raise
> my spirit to a certain indulgence in the wildest
> fantasy. All my characters and happenings are
> my creation. They don't need to coincide with
> the reality ordinary people can understand. I
> deliberately make them run counter to that
> reality. I'll gather all my emotion and ideals to
> fight against iron-strong reality.

On the one hand, we see in Can Xue's stories no
glorification of socialism, no elevation of the masses
toward some glorious ideal. Which is to say that we
cannot usefully judge her fiction by any ideological
standards of readability that put aside all literature not
immediately accessible to the Chinese masses. On the
other hand, though she is familiar with a range of
foreign authors who might provide a stay against the
ordinary (Woolf, Sartre, Beckett among them), Can
Xue has found her own manner of expression in a
transmuted desire that lends its lyricism to such a work
as "Dialogues in Paradise" and in a barely repressed
scorn that blisters her characters — siblings, spouses,
parents, neighbors — throughout the stories. Love and
anger, lyric and satire, not the political commitment
of Chinese fiction or the detached irony of much

Western modernism, are the twin impulses that power her fiction.

In a country where the sense of the ordinary is strongly enforced, a country where all are crowded into involuntary and often abrasive proximity, "My way," she has said, "is a constant deepening of the inner mind." This delving into the self is the chief characteristic of Can Xue's own idea of her work: "I am always probing myself, using nonrational methods, but I never stop at any particular point." She recognizes, and accepts, the risks that attend such an approach: "The deeper it is, the more abstract, the more weird, the more unthinkable the writing becomes. To ordinary readers, it is as difficult as deciphering some secret code. If I go on like this, I might lose all my readers. But what other ways are there? I am like this. I don't care about readers!"

It is not surprising, then, that Can Xue's work is most successful with the young and the disenchanted. Her fiction appeals to those who would stand against a stifling tradition, those who have grown discouraged, even cynical, in their quest for something real and personal. Letters from young Chinese students, teachers, and scholars reflect the mood out of which Can Xue's stories arise: "In China," one young scholar says, citing Orwell, "politics chokes literature, in one way or another, 'like tea leaves blocking a sink.' " Another, in reference to Chinese university teachers, says, "They force us to follow them. I feel miserable that I can't change it. The only thing I can do is leave; otherwise I will die." A young intellectual, reflecting on the suppression of the 1986 "Democracy Movement," remarks that "What happened during the past forty days in China will inevitably impact on Chinese literature. The school of Exploring Novels may come to an end. The younger novelists . . . may keep silence for a period, or forever. . . . As usual, after a 'political storm,' the books of antitradition more often than not disappear from the shelves. But this time, let the governors do it."[2]

The theme is an honest one, churned to the surface by the surge and flux of recent Chinese history. In 1956, for example, the Chinese Communist Party declared a period of open expression for intellectuals: "Let a hundred flowers bloom. Let a hundred schools of thought contend." In 1957 many of those who had risen to the invitation found themselves in work camps for "rectification." (Can Xue's own parents, as she tells in her memoir, were caught up in this sweep.) In 1965 the Great Proletarian Cultural Revolution commenced; by 1969 its main participants were being rusticated and set to hard labor. In 1979 the Party announced that all this had been a grievous error, and finally, cultural vertigo set in.

Many Chinese writers, most of them in their forties or fifties, have tried to capture in fiction the confusion these changing times have held for the peasant masses (Gu Hua, *A Small Town Called Hibiscus*), the university intellectuals (Dai Hou-ying, *The Stones of the Wall*), those interned on the work farms (Zhang Xianliang, *Half of Man Is Woman*), and even the Party faithful (Wang Meng, "The Butterfly"). The title of Wang's

celebrated story evokes Zhuangzi's philosophical anecdote from the fourth century B.C.:

> Once upon a time I dreamed myself a butterfly,
> floating like petals in the air, happy to be doing
> as I pleased, no longer aware of myself! But soon
> enough I awoke and then, frantically clutching
> myself, Zhuangzi was I! I wonder: was Zhuangzi
> dreaming himself the butterfly, or was the
> butterfly dreaming itself Zhuangzi?[3]

The philosopher's quandary (not unknown in the
West, of course; it appears, for example, in nearly all
of Nikos Kazantzakis's novels) serves as a metaphor in
Wang's narrative for the bewilderment of a Party cadre
who finds his "rehabilitation" just as inexplicable as his
earlier imprisonment, and the story is otherwise in-
teresting for its use of stream of consciousness, one of
the first modernist devices rediscovered for post-Maoist
fiction. But Can Xue is a younger writer than any of
these, with different interests, and she explores and
employs as the essence of her art the very dynamics
of metamorphic and oneiric processes implied in
Zhuangzi's anecdote.

Can Xue, whose real name is Deng Xiao-hua, was
born in Changsha, Hunan Province, in 1953. Her
memoir "A Summer Day in the Beautiful South" pro-
vides a moving self-portrait, an intimate view of her
family and friends, and a fascinating supplement to
the many accounts we already have of life in the past
three decades in the People's Republic of China. As
she suggests here, she began writing fiction seriously
only in 1983, when she was thirty.

The imaginative vitality of her stories is as personal as it is literary. In a letter, for example, she relates this incident from her childhood:

> I used to have a sparrow when I was a kid. It could peck rice like a chick. But my mother said it was not hygienic and threw it into the well when I was out. Later on, I raised a cat with my younger brother. I had it for years till it gave birth to kittens and was then sent away by my mother. For all this, I hated her bitterly. I even wrote her name on a roof tile and threw it into the well!

This reprisal is as magical as many moments in her fiction, bordering on voodoo or totemism. A fortune teller once told Can Xue that she was "suitable for struggle in the black society." The transforming power of magic is embedded in her experience, and in formative ways:

> I had a grandmother [the one described in the memoir] who knew a little witchcraft. She starved to death in the hard times in the 1960s. I loved her very much. She seemed neurotic and very humorous, too. She was illiterate, but she could tell all kinds of wonderful stories. She was an unyielding woman, surrounded with mystery and wonder.

At first Can Xue wrote in a diary without any thought of publication, and it was only by chance that a friend read her work and began to spread the news. "All of a sudden I became a 'writer,'" she has said. Even now her approach to writing remains casual: